Broken Umbrellas
By
Darren Arthurs

This book was only made possible by the emergence of Covid-19. It allowed me a quieter routine where I battled insomnia by mapping out and writing a story about a young boy who one day grew tired of his world and set off to find a new one.

Thank you to my wife for keeping our daughters entertained for a few hours a day so I could write.

Copyright 2020

All characters, places, names (be it people, businesses or addresses) and details are wholly fictional and any resemblance to anyone alive or dead is totally coincidental. Sure there are similarities, I know people who have utter twats for partners who would much rather spend their time on their X-Box and their money in the pub rather than looking after and raising their children but I don't think any of them are as bad as the monster I tried to come up with here. Obviously domestic abuse is something that happens in every street in every town and I hope the people in that situation someday find the strength to leave. Bullies are real and they exist no matter what your age, the bottom line is, speak up and tell people, bullies hate being seen for what they are! Anyway, I digress, this is supposed to be the legal bit.

Original cover design by author

Chapter One – Toby

At night, the family home can be a peaceful place, darkened bedrooms filled with the gentle thrum of breathing, little ones dreaming, adults laying embraced, their bodies stop waiting for the coming dawn. Maybe there is a cat downstairs asleep beneath a radiator, the family dog stretched out in its bed or on the rug, murmuring and dreaming about whatever dogs dream about. The term for this kind of scene is idyllic. But rarely do things stay that way and rarer still, do stories stay that way.
I don't want to ruin your ideas of where this story will go, and I'm not about to make bold promises that everyone in this story will have the happy ending that we wish for, but there will be moments of small triumphs. Dotted around these small islands of relief are, inevitably, moments of sadness and moments that may well make you shake your head and think uncharitable thoughts towards certain people, but do stick with it, because whatever life is, it's usually worth sticking with...

The main character of this story is Toby. Toby is a seven (nearly eight) year old boy and, like every other seven-year-old boy, is your typical seven-year-old boy, that is to say (rather confusingly) he's unlike every other seven-year-old boy because at this age, no two children are the same. Of course they all *say* they like Star Wars and Spiderman but they all pick a different favourite Star Wars character and not one of them could tell you why they liked Spiderman, some would say the suit, some the ability to swing on those strange strands that appear from his wrists and some the fact that he's cool. Being seven is a tricky time, it's when children look beyond the classroom and the garden wall and realise that there is a bigger world out there, it might not be in reach, but there is something larger looming around the corner.
Toby was one of those people. Being nearly eight meant that he had had a few more months to look at the map of the world and imagine panda's roaming free in China, cowboys riding horses in America and

you couldn't move for Giraffe's in some parts of Africa. The world was vast, vaster than anything a typical seven year old's brain could comprehend, but, like I said, Toby isn't your typical seven-year-old. Toby's story began badly and, during the course of this chapter of his life, will only slightly improve, he'll have good days and bad days like the rest of us, but ultimately his fate will be determined by the company he keeps and the decisions he makes along the way.
He was immediately put up for foster care when he was born, his mother was something that the older generation would have described as a 'good time girl', splitting her time between the benefits queue and various bars and clubs. She would go home with anyone with a nice smile and tight pair of jeans but basing your decisions on those things will lead to disaster eventually and so began a never-ending revolving door of bad man after bad man, each one leaving a deeper hole for her to climb out of. Finally, that hole was so deep that she was lost beneath layers of regret, anger, debt, alcoholism, a drug addiction. Her choice in partners went from the attractive to the unattractive and desperate. Pretty soon her benefits would not stretch to affording everything she needed. Cigarettes replaced vegetables, alcohol replaced fruit and basic food replaced the luxuries. It became more difficult to afford things like paying the bills, the new nicely scented shampoo and shower gel from the television adverts and buying birth control. Unsurprisingly, nature saw its chance and stepped in to give her something to love and care for, but a child was never on her bucket list, so once Toby arrived, Toby was placed into foster care.
For the purpose of closing the door on Toby's mothers' story, she sadly died in a car accident a few months later. Drunk and high on pills her that-day boyfriend thought he could drive like a racing driver through the town centre, he was doing very well considering the substances in his body, but brick walls are unforgiving things. Her unremarkable last words were "I love chicken burgers".

Toby's life seemed to improve significantly, placed with a foster carer who specialised in looking after very small children, Toby was kept healthy, happy and well fed. Gone was the smoke fumes and poor diet, now it was feeding on demand, no painful trapped wind and a yellow bunny called Harold. Things were looking up for young Toby, in fact these few, short months would turn out to be some of the happiest for a very long time, but no one was to know that, especially not the tubby little blonde-haired boy happily bouncing up and down over in the corner. But the downside of staying with someone who specialises in looking after very small children is, once you are too old, you get moved on. So, Toby moved to a more permanent home.

At nine months old his world became infinitely busier, now he was living on the west coast of England in a town called Weston-Super-Mare with a middle-aged couple called the Franks. They had been taking in foster children for decades and were experienced in dealing with all kinds of age groups, problems and emotions and there seemed to be a never-ceasing wave of tantrums in the Franks house. Victor and Jane Frank shared a bedroom at the rear of the house on the ground floor, this was strictly off limits to everyone in the house, they said it was because they needed a part of the house to feel theirs, this wasn't the only rule of course but people stuck by it and harmony was restored each night when the couple would climb into bed without the fear of having Lego bricks (or something much worse) awaiting them when they pulled back the covers.

The children all slept on the first floor of the house, there were two boys in one bedroom; a fourteen-year-old called Habeeb and a thirteen-year-old called Robert. Two girls shared the largest of the three bedrooms, these were Tash and Natalie, they were sisters who had been living with the Franks for a few years, Tash was ten and Natalie was twelve, Natalie was on twenty four hour hormone watch because anything could set her off and there was no telling in which direction she would fly, on a tame day she would sob uncontrollably at a charity advert on television but, on a bad day, and these seemed to becoming more and more common, she would turn angry and aggressive for no reason. These were the times when the children would either go to the garden, hide in their bedrooms or go out and when the downstairs bedroom became a place of relative safety for the carers themselves.

Toby shared with a girl of three called Millie and she would be his first real friend. He wouldn't know it in later life, but Millie adored her nine-month-old roommate, and she was as maternal and as caring as anyone could have hoped for.

I don't wish to fill each page with a tale of woe but Millie was the sole survivor of a house fire, apparently some act of revenge by a petty ex-boyfriend who understood the basic principles of making fire but forgot the golden rule that; if you start a fire, be sure you can put it out again. No one was more shocked by how quickly fire can spread on a hallway carpet more than him. It was lucky that Millie's room was directly above the front door of the house where the concrete plinth over the door acted as an ideal ledge for a neighbour to stand on while he smashed the window and pulled the screaming Millie out.

Not many children have the voice of a smoking addict, but smoke has a way of finding young windpipes, Millie does not mind, Habeeb tells her a smoky voice is cool.

Just a few months after Millie and Toby became best of friends, it was time for Toby to be introduced to a young couple called Jess and Brian. The future was looking very bright indeed for Toby, he'd been well looked after by his first carers and he'd felt real love under the doting eye of Millie and now, well now his life was about to take another turn because babies are the sought-after prize in foster children and something pulls on the heart strings when you are given the chance to make a real difference to a baby's life.

Weeks went by and Toby, Jess and Brian formed a nice bond, he even reached for Jess when she came to visit. After the usual checks by the council, everything seemed above board, Brian worked from home writing software code for different companies, he was a freelancer that could pick and choose his schedule while Jess worked at the local supermarket. The pay was not great but within a few years she could get promotion and maybe, if the mood took her, she could move to another store and perhaps do some courses in management. It was perfect. No criminal records, a steady income, someone always at home if Toby was unwell. Yes, the future was rosy, so, with all boxes ticked, Toby went to live with Jess and Brian. How I wish I could finish the story here, it would be such a fitting end to have a young boy find his new home, all tied up with a little ribbon, maybe throw in a pet puppy along the way, birthday parties, best friends, learning to ride a bike, a first kiss. But no. Toby must do a few more things yet until he can truly be happy.

Chapter Two – 19 Brook Gardens

Brook Gardens probably brings about thoughts of grandeur, a lovely street with picturesque green spaces where children can safely play, neighbours greet each other with a warm hello and will kindly take your bins in if you're late home from work one evening. That is not the case, although Brook Gardens is an ok place to live, what I described rarely exists anymore.

Jess and Brian live in a modest three bed terraced house, to one side is a single man who does God knows what for a living and is almost never seen, he comes and goes at all hours of the day and night, Jess describes him as someone that likes to keep himself to himself but he's one of those men who dies with millions of pounds in the bank and a secret family in Thailand that nobody has ever heard of yet they appear at the funeral to gasps and shock from the lifelong friends in attendance.

Jess likes to make up little stories for the people she meets and sees, it's never malicious or done with spite but we all see people that we meet regularly that we know nothing about, what's the harm in making up our own backstory?

The other side is Jim and Cath, a retired couple. Jim used to work for the National Trust and Cath was a school teacher, both are pretty hard of hearing - something that you will need to remember for later on, the things that go on in Jess and Brian's house would have been acted upon by someone who was at home regularly or had a normal level of hearing. They are the far nicer neighbours out of the pairing, keen gardeners they can often be seen pottering away in the garden and enjoying their retirement together.

Brian is more regimented and serious than Jess, you could argue that is what makes their relationship a strong one, their ability to complement each other. Brian takes care of the running of the house, the bills, the better deals on insurance and all that grown up stuff, while Jess works, cooks, cleans and looks after Toby. Some would say this is a boring existence, but others would jump at the chance of having such a mundane life.

There seems to be a trend for seizing the day, people cry "carpe diem" before jumping out of a plane, that's all well and good but you can't "live everyday like it's your last", no matter what the advertising men advise, it's just not practical. The best we can hope for is for a few weeks a year where we remove ourselves from the typical working week and do something for us. Mundane pays the bills as an old friend of mine used to say and it is difficult to argue with that logic.

Toby learnt to walk at 19 Brook Gardens, it was in that very living room that he staggered up on his little bowed legs and took his first steps, clutching the sofa for support he toddled and tumbled but was cheered on by his loving parents before doing it again and again until he could easily traverse the downstairs rooms. Jess used to miss the days when she could put him somewhere and have full faith that when she turned to check on him, he would still be there. Those days were gone she used to say to herself, soon he will be pulling at the stairgate wanting to tackle the stairs, she would double check the lock on the gate every time she passed. She had never noticed how many things in the house were dangerous, pointy things, hot things, hard things, slippery things and do not even think about the electricity. It is enough to drive a first-time parent mad. Her mother had always said "you'll think differently when you've got kids of your own" and she was bloody right. A different instinct kicks in when you've got a little human trotting around the house intent on causing mischief, it's a wonder more accidents aren't caused at home, how do children get through childhood with so much stuff around them to cause harm?

With that thought Jess closed the gate leading into the kitchen.

When Toby's first birthday came around there was no shortage of well-wishers, Jess and Brian's respective families had travelled down from the north of the country and were eager to see their new addition. It was decided from the off that Toby would be introduced to the families as a foster child, the couple had tried IVF but it was too expensive to continue and they decided that, morally, it was selfish of them to try to play God while there were so many children needing the home life they were certain they could provide. Other couples somehow saw shame in taking on foster children like it was second best, as if they had failed to fall pregnant so they opted for the next best thing. What rot! The ability to care for another child as if it's your own is what makes us human, it takes a great deal of courage and heart to do it, the step Jess and Brian took was a selfless one and their families had two choices; either accept it, or lump it. Luckily, nobody chose the latter.

Jim and Cath from next door popped round for a piece of cake and a cup of coffee, they spent a few hours chatting about their garden and their plans for the following year, it was nearing time to sow more seeds in Jim's small green house at the foot of the garden. People from Jim's generation happily chatted away, comparing plants and trees and stories of failed vegetable growth, while the younger people thought it was silly talk and stared at their phones and took photos of Toby. It was a day for the photo albums and one that went a long way in building a stronger bonder between the young family.

There is something very social about having a baby in a buggy, you seem to bump into the same people, you share hellos and goodbyes and, on the occasion you meet another mother pushing her child around in a buggy, you can share concerns or worries and war stories involving vomit, dirty nappies and embarrassing mishaps. Before long, you create a small network of people in the same position. You offer advice on feeding, weening, what products to buy, knowledge on all manners of creams, lotions and potions and suddenly the world is a larger place. Everyone, it seems, has a baby too!

Add to this the long line of people with a dog that you happen to meet whilst out walking and your world has grown considerably. Not bad for someone who, up until the arrival of Toby, could count her friends on one hand (and Brian made up a third of them).

Life for Jess was changing by the hour, she had a child to care for, a husband to care for and a growing number of social commitments that she didn't want to miss, it was good for Toby to socialise with children nearby, he even made a friend that he liked to play with, a little girl called Josie who, although smack bang in the midst of the terrible two's enjoyed the companionship that the calm-natured Toby brought. Her mother used to joke that the only things that could calm Josie down was Peppa Pig, Toby and Jack Daniels, the ladies laughed awkwardly unsure whether there was any truth in the Jack Daniels bit, they all secretly convinced themselves there wasn't but you never know...

Brian grew more and more removed from Jess and Toby, it was not as if he was cold or aloof, he just wasn't there as much. Choosing instead to work in the small bedroom that they turned into an office complete with desk, chair, various shelves with files on and a small fern that was given to him by Jim when upon hearing Brian worked from home. He told him plants were good for the brain and if every office worker had a plant each then carbon emissions would be zero, or something like that, Brian was too busy looking at the plant to let his ears take in the information fully. He was like that, you could be talking to him and his mind would visibly wander, as if his brain had decided to go off and think about something else while you wittered on about the weather or something equally as uninteresting.

For months this went on, the daily routine of Jess waking, seeing to Toby, grabbing breakfast and witnessing her husband come into their life, grab a coffee, give Toby a kiss on the forehead, grab some toast, kiss Jess on the forehead and go upstairs before the keys of his keyboard would start tapping leaving Jess and Toby for a few moments before she went to work.

Toby would play on the landing mostly, just out of sight of Brian, but a quick glance to his right would put Toby in full view. He would spend time in his room chasing a ball or throwing Harold (his yellow rabbit) up into the air. One of his favourite pastimes was sliding underneath his bed and saying "Toby?" over and over in his broken speech. This would cause him no end of enjoyment, especially if

Harold was in sight, perhaps Toby thought Harold was calling him, who knows, but Toby wasn't what you would call a needy child, he was happy to play alone or to simply watch you go about your business.

It is funny how a life can find a routine, how it can fall into a groove that, over time becomes deeper and deeper until anything out of the ordinary, no matter how simple or mundane, seems unthinkable. It was not long until Brian's behaviour became the norm, and he would spend more time on his own than with Jess and Toby. Of course, it did not *feel* like he was breaking away from the family, it happened so slowly and gradual that it almost felt like evolution. Jess would find herself making excuses to her family why Brian couldn't come to the phone or why he wasn't able to visit one summer, eventually it became a joke and her family would say things like "I suppose Brian's too busy to talk? He really should take a break" and was simply dismissed. But on the rare occasion that Jess would think and secretly question what was going on, she decided to not dwell on it and to let things run their course. She was convinced he wasn't having an affair, there were no tell-tale signs, he wouldn't suddenly have to go out, he wasn't spending time on his phone away from her or receiving strange texts from unknown numbers and he wasn't acting suspicious, he just wasn't around as much as he used to be, or she wanted him to be.

Jim next door suggested he might be having some kind of 'episode'. She'd heard about these things happening to men, but that tended to happen later in life, it was commonly called a mid-life crisis and it typically occurred when a man realised their best years were behind them and they had an almost uncontrollable urge to relive their youth. Sometimes this involved a new hobby or clothes and could spiral out of control on the much- documented sports car and a blonde – much younger – girlfriend. But Brian was not the type to ogle at a shiny sports car or look longingly at a twenty-year-old woman. It was fine. They'd spoken about this a few weeks ago and Brian had told her that he had decided to try to reach the 'next level' in his education so was trying to balance his work load with a couple

of online courses that would open a few doors. It was hard work but wouldn't be forever and the extra knowledge would mean more money coming in and, eventually him having to do less work for the same pay, leaving him to spend more time with her and Toby.
Another birthday came and went for our little hero, on turning two years old he changed overnight, it was like a ban had been lifted and suddenly he was allowed to throw tantrums, shout, stomp his feet and generally be a pain in the arse. He would still lay under his bed but now he would refuse to come out if the mood took him, it was common for Jess to come home from work to find Brian on all fours in Toby's bedroom, his head under the bed pleading with the boy to come out. To his eternal credit Brian never lost his temper, he would make a game out of it and tell him that there was a group of trolls downstairs stealing the cereal and he was too big and clumsy to catch them, if only Toby would come out, he could catch them and they could rescue the food. Sometimes this worked, sometimes it did not and sometimes, just sometimes, Toby would hide under his bed *wanting* his dad to ask for his help. Life is one big game when you're two years old, when your best friend is a yellow rabbit, and you get to be the hero in your own story.

It was one such day that Jess, upon returning home was greeted by the sound of Brian shouting at Toby, she closed the front door with a level of confusion, this had never happened before, whatever Brian was shouting for must be serious. Taking off her coat and putting her bag on the sofa she made her way to the stairs, it was clear that they were in Toby's room but that normally meant playtime, not an argument.

"Toby, just give me the phone" she heard Brian say.

Standing on the stairs, she could look through the handrail and into Toby's room, there was Brian, in the classic pose of all fours, and she could see Toby's feet. He was under his bed but curled away against the wall, as far from Brian as he could get.

"The phone!" Brian said, his voice raised.

Jess took the few last remaining steps and entered the room, "what's going on?" she asked "Toby, are you ok?"

Brian got up and gave Jess a frustrated look, "he's playing silly buggers, he took my phone and then sprinted in here and hid under his bed, he's been here for ages. It's driving me mad."
Jess and Brian swapped positions, Brian stood, and Jess peered under the bed.
"Are you ok little man?" she asked gently.
"Is HE ok?!" Brian shouted.
Jess looked up and told Brian that he was scaring him. Brian gave her a look of utter bewilderment and stormed out of the room.
"What happened Tobes?" asked Jess.
Toby was backed up against the wall, looking frightened and a little confused, she could not see Brian's phone anywhere.
"Come on – she said – Out you come" she offered a hand and Toby took it and started to wriggle out from his hiding place.
As he got closer Jess could see Brian's phone, it was behind Toby all the time, even if Toby wanted to give it back, he wouldn't have been able to, he was pressing it up against the wall. Just as Jess was hugging the frightened toddler, Brian's phone started vibrating.
"Ooh Toby, grab daddy's phone"
In Jess's mind she was thinking Toby could return it to Brian and hopefully the whole issue would be put to bed, or at least until she could talk to Brian about it later when Toby was put to bed. It was clear something was niggling him; he had not reacted like that before, maybe he had taken too much on with the new workload.
Toby handed her the phone, the display informed her that someone called 'Ceal' was calling. It was not a name she recognised, but that was not anything new, he got phone calls quite regularly and this did not seem any different or arouse suspicion.
It would not be long until it went through to answer machine, so Jess decided to answer on Brian's behalf.
"Hello? This is...."
Jess was interrupted by an American voice, she spoke very loosely, she was obviously familiar with Brian. A woman can pick up on this kind of thing immediately, in those brief few seconds, Jess learnt a great deal about Ceal and not all of it was encouraging.

Rudely, Jess hung up the phone. For some reason things felt odd, something had changed, she felt as if the windows had been opened and a new view had been revealed. It was nonsense she told herself, Brian is always at home. Always. At. Home.

She opened the call log of Brian's phone and the name Ceal appeared quite a few times, scrolling down it told her that Ceal called Brian once every one or two days, they were obviously engaging in long conversations, the shortest was eight minutes. But this was normal, clients would sometimes contact Brian often, checking up on him, asking for updates, reporting glitches about the software he had written, she was being silly.

But the seed was there, and it began to grow in Jess's mind.

Life continued as normal within the small terraced walls of 19 Brook Garden, Toby was continuing to develop, his social skills were getting better, he enjoyed playing and was slowly but surely showing signs of confidence and intelligence, all encouraging things. Jess was doing well at work, her decision to take on more responsibility was met with appreciation from here bosses and Brian continued to work hard in his small study, things were pretty rosy, until the evening. Toby was not yet versed in reading the body language and hidden messages that people often sneak into their vocabulary through sarcasm or plain lies, but he could sense something wasn't quite right.

Dinner times were tense, and the conversations were never easy and loose, often throwaway remarks were met with "and what do you mean by that?" from Jess. It all culminated one summers evening when, upon hearing sudden loud noises – that eventually Toby would recognise as slamming doors – Toby was awoken by his squabbling parents. A child of his age has no understanding of the complications of the typical adult relationship, but he knew immediately something was very wrong. It appeared that Brian had come out of his and Jess's bedroom at quite some speed, he then stomped downstairs, pulled open the small cupboard that sits beneath the stairs, and pulled something out. All this was going on while Jess was saying confusing things like "oh yes, that's right!" and "what is *that* going to solve" and the worrying "where will you go?" (which Brian replied loudly with "what do you care?!"). Toby had never known anything like this, he had heard thunderstorms in the past, he didn't particularly like them but Jess assured him that it was something to do with God tidying his kitchen in heaven and Brian had said it was something to do with what makes the television and the lights work. It was all very confusing but because they did not seem worried by it, he was not. Even Harold, his yellow bunny, seemed unmoved, which was a little strange given that Harold was quite jumpy and would often go to bed next to Toby only to be found under the bed come the morning. This was like a thunderstorm but indoors. Maybe Brian was trying to find something to put the storm in, the under stairs cupboard had the vacuum cleaner and Brian's bag that he took to the gym, maybe the storm was so small it could fit in that bag and Brian will just pick it up and take it outside, a little like what they did with bugs and insects that came into the house.

It was not until the morning that Toby realised that Brian took the storm outside but had decided to go somewhere with it. Toby secretly hoped it did not mean that the television would not work again, he liked the television and, according to Jess, he liked the television a little *too* much.

A few days went by and Jess finally broke the news to Toby about where Brian was and when he was coming home. The conversation was a mix of grown up talk and little words that Toby could understand but the gist of it was Brian had been talking to a seal and would not be around as much as before. Toby knew exactly what was going on, he might have only been a few weeks from his third birthday, but he was nobody's fool and he wanted to make his mum happy, so he put his arm around her to comfort her. It turned out it was a stupid thing to do because immediately after he'd done it, she started to cry, he was often called a strong boy from his mum's friends but he didn't know he was *that* strong. He didn't like seeing his mum crying, he knew it had something to do with his dad but he couldn't feel angry towards him, he likes his dad, he likes his mum, it was strange not having him here and, if what his mum said was true, that he wouldn't be seeing him as much, well that was making him feel sad too.

He felt like crying, felt like shouting and felt so confused because all he could think about was why his dad had wanted to go away with a seal. He had seen them on television and in books, and admittedly they always looked cute, but they ate fish. Brian did not like fish, so what would he do for food?

Chapter Three – Three minus one

When people look back on their lives they more often than not can pick out certain times by a certain landmark, they call these times 'periods', there are some famous periods throughout history, Picasso had his blue period, David Bowie had his Ziggy Stardust period and countless people had a University period where they ate baked beans from tins and watched daytime tv in their pyjamas. This story is now entering the period that Toby, if he would have recognised it at the time, would have called it 'the calm before the storm'. These days quickly became weeks and months, which, as eventually turned into years. The house was in a never-ending evolution, first there were the regular visits from Brian, then the constant questioning from Jess towards Brian and something that she used to call his 'arrangements'. Toby just liked seeing his dad and felt the air change when that word came up, he once asked what it meant, and his mum told him it was her asking his dad where he was sleeping and who with. His dad always avoided this question, Toby couldn't understand at first, to him it was easy to answer, he sleeps upstairs in his room with Harold, apart from the odd occasion when his mum goes out and Toby is allowed to stay up to watch television with Jemma, the babysitter who smells like burnt toast and lip balm. On those nights he falls asleep on the sofa but wakes up in his bed. Near Harold. Once, come the morning, Harold was still downstairs on the sofa, so whatever they were watching must have been unmissable.
Toby had seen where seals sleep though, they slept on rocks or beaches, so he figured his dad slept there. But why not just say it? Eventually he figured that his dad was worried that his mum would make fun of him, people make fun of other people for all kinds of things, he'd seen it at nursery, no one was safe and sometimes people made fun of you for nothing that you could understand, life was strange and it didn't really make much sense.

More birthdays came and went, he didn't see as many people as before, a few of the older people were missing, his mum told him that they either couldn't make the journey because they were getting old or, sadly, some of them had died. He understood dying, it was the opposite of living and you were either one or the other, you could not be both because that was something called a zombie and they did not exist.

On his fifth birthday his dad came, and the house suddenly went very quiet because he had a girl with him who Toby had never seen before. She was very nice, quite tall and, from what he could see, she was very pretty because everyone was looking at her the whole time, the ladies in the room couldn't take their eyes off of her, she must be a lovely person. Mum did not seem very happy, but she smiled too, it was a different smile, one Toby had not seen his mum do before, her mouth made the correct shape, but her eyes seemed sad. He would have dwelled on this further if it were not for the small matter of presents to open. Whilst he unwrapped his gifts, he noticed his mum and dad walk into the kitchen away from everyone else, they looked very serious.

"I hope they haven't burnt the cake" he thought to himself.

He looked at Harold for his thoughts, but Harold just looked up at the ceiling. Typical, he was no use in a crisis.

When his mum and dad reappeared, his dad made a beeline for Toby and handed him his presents, one was large and one was quite small, obviously the large one was the interesting one. The small one was a clock with one long hand, everyone called it a compass and it was used for finding out where you were going. Apparently, it was something called 'handy', all the men agreed and nodded approvingly at this gift. Jim was a great fan of the compass, he started telling a story about his compass and the places he went with one, suddenly everyone had a tale to tell and they shared them whilst eating the cake.

Another birthday, another wish to make and another step closer to the upcoming storm.

Dad told him that the woman he was with was called Celia and lived in a country called Canada, he took Toby's compass and knelt down beside him. He said if the red half of the long hand was on the 'N' of the compass, then Canada was towards the 'W'. Brian stood up and, placing his hands-on Toby's shoulders, he turned him around until he was facing the right way. This made little sense to Toby, but he liked the compass and it would find a home safely underneath his pillow from that night onwards (well, until the storm came, storms tend to blow things away).

"Would you like to visit Canada someday Toby?" Brian asked quietly. "Uh-huh" Toby answered. Canada could have been at the bottom of a volcano or at the peak of Mount Everest for all Toby knew, but it was often better to agree to everything and then decide if it was a mistake later. He'd learnt this the hard way when he was invited to something called Laser-Battle, it was his friend George's birthday party and George had told him they all got to run around pretending to be spacemen and shooting lasers. This sounded quite good to Toby, so he told Jess he would go, if he'd have known it was going to be in a sweaty dark room with loud music and flashing lights, he might have given it a miss. For what seemed like an eternity, he was chased around by older children with serious anger issues, his 'armour' was heavy and too big so when he ran he kept knocking his thighs on the bottom of the chest plate that started vibrating and making strange noises every time he was shot. Which happened every few seconds.

But he was undeterred, Canada sounded friendly enough, apparently bears live there and most of the country is a forest, like that place in 'Return of The Jedi', maybe the bears were just as friendly, but he doubted it, he was told by his teacher at school that although bears make good toys for young children, in nature they're frightening animals that would happily chase you and give you to their cubs. But his dad and Celia would keep him safe, I doubt either of them would like to go in the forest for too long.

Canada was a subject that continued to crop up at various times, Jess had shown him where Canada was on his globe, it didn't look too far away, and, when Brian would visit, he would start talking about a place called Van Koover, which was a city in Canada where Celia lived. It did not take long before Toby worked out that maybe the reason Brian was talking about this Van Koover was because he wanted to live there with Cel.. hang on, Celia, Celia, CELia, SEALIA, SEAL? This was the seal he went to live with!

"Yes, that's right – said his mum when Toby had asked her about it – Seal is short for Celia, your Dad wanted to spend more time with her."

Toby was rather proud how he had worked this out, admittedly it took a long time but he can't be blamed for that, adults rarely make sense at the best of times, let alone when they try to confuse you by using special code names.

Jess carried on and told him how they had decided to split up, she explained how Brian had spent more and more time talking to Celia and, eventually, he wanted to move in with her. She was straight and honest and said words Toby had never heard before, things like solicitor, mortgage and custody, other words he had heard about, divorce was the main one, he knew what that was, a few children in his class had told him about divorce and it sounded scary because you end up having two bedrooms, new people in your life and mum and dad didn't seem to be friends anymore. One of his friends had not seen his dad in ages because the fights between his mum and dad were so nasty that neither wanted to see the other, this meant he only got to see his mum. But it was ok, he used to say, because none of it was my fault and my mum loves me still. He used to get presents on his birthday and at Christmas but those started either arriving late through the post, or as was the case last Christmas, he didn't get anything at all. Not even a phone call.

Divorce sounded unfair, he preferred it when his mum and dad were both with him, but Jess told him that things were ok and they were just going to start a new adventure, that sounded good to Toby, he liked adventures and, if Brian could come and say hello regularly, they'd be just fine.

Chapter four – Dean

School was going well, his teacher had told his mum that Toby was 'above the curve' when it came to his learning and social interaction, he made friends easily and never got upset when people would refuse to play with him. Tantrums were practically none existent and his behaviour was something called exemplary, he didn't know what that meant exactly but it must have been good because when his mum heard that word, she looked at Toby and smiled broadly. Whatever Toby was doing, it was making his mum very happy. If further proof was needed it came in the form of ice cream after his dinner when they returned from parents evening.

Brian had moved away with Celia to Van Koover and he sent cards and letters often, either through the post addressed to Toby personally, or through email to Jess. According to his mum, dad was also sending some money for Toby's future that was being put into a bank account that they had set up as soon as Toby came to live with them, he didn't know how much was in there but he knew it would be millions of pounds, people spoke about thousands and millions all the time, so he must have lots of money in there by now. If Jim and Cath next door could afford to give him ten pounds for his birthday and another ten pound every Christmas imagine the pile of money he was receiving from people in his family.

Yes, Toby was doing well at school, eating ice cream and had a stack of money in the bank.

It was a few weeks before his sixth birthday that a new name suddenly entered the house, someone called Dean began to feature in Jess's conversation. Jemma had been looking after Toby much more often and Jess had been spending time with Dean. Jess seemed to brighten when she spoke about him, it was totally different to the way she spoke about Brian. Toby knew all about boyfriends, Bryony at school kept asking him if he would be her boyfriend, he wasn't completely opposed to the idea but from he saw on the television boyfriends were expected to kiss their girlfriends and that wasn't something he wanted to do. Maybe he'd wait until he was seven or eight years old, his dad told him to do something that involved keeping her keen but because he was laughing when he said it, he knew his dad was joking. Plus, he did not know what keen actually was.

Celia would sometimes appear on the screen when dad would video call, he thought Celia was really nice, it was obvious his dad was happy in Canada, apart from having a beard he seemed much like he did when he lived with Toby and his mum, he knew better than to say that to mum though, mum didn't really like talking about dad and Celia, Jim next door said his mum was still sad that his dad had left. He also said that sometimes it can take years to get over something like that, but he kept reminding Toby that it was not his fault. This is what George was told. Up until this point Toby had never even suspected that his mum and dad breaking up *was* his fault, how *could* it be his fault, what had he done? Sure, he wasn't perfect, he'd done some things that he wasn't particularly proud of, there was the time when they went swimming and just a few minutes after getting into the pool he decided he needed to go to the toilet, but he told Brian very calmly so nobody could hear and they went off together. No harm done. Then there was the time he wanted an Easter egg from the shop and his mum told him no. Yes, he stomped and shouted, his mum told her friends that he had a 'total meltdown', but it did not seem important enough for someone to move to the country with the bears. Jim had suddenly made him question a few things but from what he could see his dad was happy with Celia and his mum was happy spending time with Dean. With any luck Dean would be just as nice as his dad was and then things would be back to how it was before all this trouble started.

Toby's mum spent the morning rushing around the house tidying and putting things in cupboards, Toby was watching the television, his favourite programme was on, it was a show that his dad had told him about and a certain episode featured the forests of Canada. He thought it would be interesting for Toby to see the forests and understand where his dad was living. He'd watched it with his mum but she was busy on her phone and would keep getting up to check the cooking of their dinner so she missed most of it but Toby found it the most exciting thing he'd ever seen.

It showed a man walking through the forests picking up leaves and plants and explaining what these things were, he kept putting things in his mouth and describing how they tasted. A few times Toby was forced to look away, and he spent a chunk of the programme wincing at the different things that the man ate. He showed you how to start a fire, how to make somewhere to sleep and how to make things out of wood and grass to catch small animals to eat on his fire. He kept talking about the importance of clean water, he would put his water bottle in streams and rivers and would carefully tip big leaves to catch rain water that had been trapped, it would run into his water bottle, it was brilliant.

Mum was vacuuming the lounge for the second time and kept saying how she still had a whole list of jobs to do before 'he' came.

Dean was visiting in the afternoon, mum had decided to do a barbeque and they would eat outside so Toby could meet Dean but not feel trapped, he could go and play in the garden as usual if things got boring, but Toby was excited too, he'd asked who Dean was, where he lived, if he had children, if he knew how to start a fire or trap fish in a net made out of long grass. His mum had chuckled and answered what she could but she didn't think Dean was much of a fisherman, he used to play music for people at parties and would come into the shop to talk to her. This made his mum very happy; she gave him the same smile that she did at parents evening, it was obvious Dean was a nice man.

Toby could not wait.

His first impressions of Dean were positive, Dean seemed to touch and kiss his mum much more than his dad used to, he was constantly touching her around her waist and on her bum, this was something Toby had never seen before. It had been a long time since he'd seen anybody kiss his mum, he guessed it was normal to them both, but to him, it was still strange, but his mum seemed to be smiling and laughing so it couldn't be a bad thing.

The barbeque went well, Toby probably ate too much food, but nobody seemed to mind or notice, Toby wasn't what you would describe as a greedy child, he knew if you ate lots of food but didn't move around enough you would get heavier and heavier until the doorframes would need to be widened, his mum didn't have enough money to pay a builder to come around and change the door frames, and his dad didn't send enough money to pay for it, so he ate until he was full and then stopped. It seemed on this particular day, two burgers, a sausage and a dollop of coleslaw was enough to make him stop.

One thing he noticed though was that Dean seemed to have a problem with tomato ketchup. Not only did he not put any ketchup on his own food, he also seemed to be annoyed that Toby put it on his food and, when he went to get more, Dean moved the bottle away and said "I think you've got enough sauce on your plate there mate".

Mum did not hear this, she was helping herself to some more salad, but the way Dean said it sounded like he was serious. Toby didn't like that; he wanted the ketchup, and it wasn't as if anybody else was going to eat it. Toby went quiet and returned to eating his lunch.

That evening, after Dean had gone – it took him ages to go, he kept kissing his mum and they spent ages standing at the door saying goodbye – Toby stood at the top of the garden chatting to Cath and Jim.

"So, how was mum's boyfriend?" asked Jim.

"He was ok." Toby answered, his mum had told him that people need a bit of getting used to and sometimes it takes time before you really like someone, Toby thought he would be wiser to wait until Dean had visited a few times. There was no point in doing something called gossiping, people told tales at school and nobody liked that, they were the unpopular children in the class.

"Your mum must like him. I imagine since your dad left, she's felt quite lonely looking after you on her own, I think it's good for her to meet someone. It could be good for you too." Added Cath.

They were tidying the garden and putting things away in their shed. The shed is touching distance from Toby's garden and he often sits at the top away from the house where he can play in peace, there is a space between a crumbled low wall and the thick hedge that borders the garden to the rear, it's been a place where Toby can hide away or hide things away since he moved there. It has been the final resting place for many a toy car or action figure. One day archaeologists may dig up this area and find these items. Future scholars will wonder at the strange civilisation that admired vehicles and soldiers so much that they made miniature replicas of them, people will come from miles around to view the artefacts and the crisp packets and juice cartons that were found alongside these novelties.

"He wouldn't let me have any tomato ketchup" Toby said slowly, he looked down towards the house to make sure his mum wasn't in earshot, she was tidying the things away and was visible through the kitchen window as she was cleaning the plates and bowls from the barbeque.

"Who? Dean?" Asked Cath.

Toby nodded.

"To be fair Toby, you do eat a lot of it. I'm always seeing tomato ketchup around your mouth or on you tee shirt". Added Jim.

"It always drips down my front' Toby said looking at the floor.

"Perhaps if you didn't waste so much by wearing it, you wouldn't need more."

Cath had a point, he did lose rather a lot by not having it reach his mouth, maybe he should try harder not to spill so much.

Dean visited 19 Brook Gardens more and more, he would come for meals once or twice a week and sometimes they would visit somewhere at the weekend. Toby had a blue scooter that he would zoom around on, it had matching blue wheels and when the steepness of the path was correct and no one was coming in the opposite direction, he could go so fast that his eyes would water and he would have a funny feeling in his tummy. His mum used to call to him to slow down but he would pretend he couldn't hear her and carry on anyway, he liked the way the wind suddenly had a sound and the thrum of the wheels travelled up through his legs making his voice tremble when he spoke.

He liked all kinds of wheels; he saw bigger children at the park standing on little pieces of wood and whooshing around on tiny wheels. His mum called them skateboards and they seemed a lot of fun, occasionally someone would fall off one and the children would say swears, one boy had a blooded knee that looked really painful, Toby couldn't stop looking at it. That boy would need to wash it and put some moss in the cut, he'd seen that on the television, you need to keep cuts clean because you can get something called an infection in it. If you get a really bad infection things turn black and you have to chop parts of you off. Luckily the people where Toby live are clever and keep cuts clean because he hadn't seen many people with legs missing yet but older children, particularly boys, were typically silly and if anyone was going to lose a leg, it was them. Toby would stick to his scooter for the time being until he could get a bigger bike.

He had learnt to ride a bike a few months before, but his bike was too small, he kept hitting the handlebars with his knees if he turned a corner and it made him fall off. His mum said they would try and get him a bigger bike, but he would have to wait until the scooter became too small. He did not mind that, he liked his scooter and it meant he could scoot alongside his mum when she went jogging, a bike would be too fast for her, she wouldn't manage to keep up with him.

Dean would come to the park on the odd occasion but he was always hurrying Toby up, he would stand with his mum and call things like "ok Toby two more minutes and we need to go" and "one more go then mate", it was really off putting and a little embarrassing when Toby was playing a game of tag with some other children and suddenly Dean was calling stupid things out. Mum never did that; she would sit on a bench with other mums and hold Toby's coat while he conquered the climbing frame or tackled the monkey bars. He was not a fan of the swings, he was more of a climber, sitting down while you went back and forwards only held a limited appeal. No, fun was climbing ladders and jumping over things and he had a favourite park, he liked it so much he made a promise that he would never invite Dean there, he would ruin it. Mum can still go there of course, but Dean? No.

After a while Toby's mum asked if they could have a chat, Toby suspected something was wrong, she had fish fingers for tea, alarm bells always rang when fish fingers were put in the oven. His school friend George was the same, George's mum fed him fish fingers when she told him that he was going to have a stepbrother, so what was mum going to say?

"Toby, how would feel about Dean coming to live with us?"

At this exact point, something amazing happened, totally unrelated but rather symbolic all the same, a sudden crash of thunder boomed high above in the sky.

Jess looked around the room and commented what strange timing it was, "sounds like the start of a storm" she said smiling.

If only they knew.

Chapter Five – The King in The Castle

When things change, it can take a while to understand the extent of those changes, sometimes they can be good, some are even welcomed and can lead to a new way of living and behaving.
 The arrival of Dean started off well, the house was a little fuller of life and things did not change for a few weeks. It was gradual at first, an outsider looking in would not have seen any reason to be concerned or worried. Toby still had his mum around, his dad was a phone, or video, call away and Dean had his own routine to stick to with work, he worked on building sites doing something called plastering, in Toby's mind Dean went into new houses and put a type of thick paint on the walls so the walls were smooth and ready to paint any colour the new owners wanted. He always came home covered in drips of white crusty stuff, but his mum was happy and would kiss him and tell him to go and get changed. Toby had his own space and Dean had his, they did not share much time together but what they shared was their love for his mum and, as long as she was happy, he was happy.
The first big change was Toby's bedroom, no longer was the second biggest bedroom his, his mum had an idea that Toby might feel happier in the small room, his dad's old office. She told him that it made sense for the smallest person to have the smallest room and Toby couldn't really argue with that, he understood what she meant and it was a waste of that room having his dad's old desk and chair in there, Toby could move in there and they could make it really nice for him. But wasn't his room already nice anyway?
The truth, Toby suspected, was that Dean wanted that room for himself. Dean stayed in his mum's room, so why did he need two rooms?
Toby asked this one evening over dinner and noticed that every time his mum was about to answer, she would look at Dean.
"We thought you would like the small room; you can look out onto the garden from there and you won't get the noise from the road.

It's important, now you're getting older, to get a good night sleep." She said.
Toby thought about this for a few seconds, he was not very good at compromise, seven-year olds rarely are.
"I don't want to move. I like where I am."
"That's a bit selfish mate" Dean said, he gave his mum a look that Toby didn't recognise, it was almost as if Dean was making excuses for him, as if Dean was saying sorry to his mum for Toby's behaviour. The cheek!
Toby didn't give a stuff if Dean thought he was being selfish, Dean was the new comer, if he liked that small room so much then he was welcome to stay in there in his clothes that looked like a flock of birds had pooed on him. If he were braver and older, he would have told him that there and then, he would have stood up, told him and walked away with a handful of chips. Or, better still, he would have sat back down calmly and carried on with his sausage and chips leaving Dean to walk away.
But the truth was, he wasn't brave or older, but he also didn't want to move rooms, he liked his bigger room and moving to a smaller room meant his things wouldn't fit in there so his things would be in two rooms, which wasn't very practical.
"I won't be able to fit all of my things into the small room" he said. He knew big things do not fit into small spaces; he had learnt this at school.
"We'd have a clear out of things, you've got lots of toys you don't play with anymore." Said his mum.
"Would we get new toys?" Toby asked, suddenly this offer was tempting.
"Of course -said his mum again smiling – isn't that right Dean?"
"Absolutely" said Dean looking at Toby. But he did not smile. No, Dean did not smile very much at all towards Toby.
If Toby was a paranoid child, he would have spent hours and hours wondering about Dean's feelings towards him, but he wasn't, Dean was simply mum's boyfriend and the one who made him move rooms and wave goodbye to some of his old toys. Apparently, they

were going to the charity shop for other boys and girls to enjoy, this didn't make Toby feel particularly good about things, all it meant was someone else, a stranger, was going to be playing with his toys now. In a few short weeks, Dean had moved in, had convinced his mum that Toby should move out of his room and at dinner time the ketchup was nowhere to be seen, if Toby had some with his dinner, it was squirted onto the plate and put back into the cupboard, Toby initially used to ask for more ketchup but if his mum ever rose from her chair to get it, Dean would put his hand on her arm and say it wasn't good for Toby and she should stay and enjoy her meal. Sometimes she would say it was fine and get it, but Dean would sulk, that's right he would sulk like the boys in Toby's class at school. Toby knew what sulking looked like (he did it himself on the odd occasion) and Dean was a sulker. Normally sulking didn't work with his mum, she would stick to her guns and you could sulk all day and all night and she wouldn't budge or change her mind, you may as well give up because sulking wasn't going to get the job done, but when Dean did it, it was a different matter, it worked for him. He would immediately go quiet, this was no bother to Toby, he preferred it when Dean was quiet, it meant more time for Toby to talk about places he wanted to go to on holiday and things he wanted to do when he got older. He looked at the ketchup bottle and wonder why it was called ketchup when brown sauce was called brown sauce, why isn't ketchup called red sauce and why are most sauces brown but not called brown sauce too? Gravy was brown, barbeque sauce was brown but they were called other things, he thought whoever it was that first invented brown sauce simply had no imagination or had other sauces they were trying to invent that were different colours, did that mean somewhere there was a blue sauce or a green sauce? He thought this as he was eating his sausage and chips and chasing rogue peas around the plate. One of the peas rolled off the plate and onto the table.

"He even eats like a baby" said Dean.

Toby looked up at him, what a strange thing to say, Toby hadn't seen many babies eat but from what he could gather babies were much worse than him, they used their hands for a start and smeared most of their food around their faces. This Dean was a strange person, and it slowly dawned on Toby that maybe Dean was not someone he could become a fan of.

"He eats fine – said his mum – peas have a mind of their own, don't they Tobes?"

Toby nodded, picked up the pea with his fingers and ate it.

Later that evening Toby was in his (smaller) bedroom, sitting on his bed, holding Harold while his mum was running the bath down the corridor. He had just his socks and pants on and was daydreaming while he looked around the room. He did not notice the approach of Dean.

"This is a much better room, a little room for a little prince" he said leaning against the door frame and looking up at the corners.

"I don't have room for my table" Toby said looking at him. He noticed how tall Dean was, and, from where he was sitting, he could see a part of a tattoo peeking out from underneath Dean's t-shirt.

"You don't need a table, why would you need a table? We've got one downstairs." He asked.

"I can keep my books and paper on it."

"You've got a table at school, don't you?" Dean sneered.

Toby nodded and looked at Harold, who, as usual, was little or no support.

"There you go then, waste of time having two tables. You don't need that big room, I've got some things I need to put in there, some private things and I don't want you going in there right?" he asked, but Toby recognised that kind of question, it's not a question to be argued with.

Jess was fussing around in the bathroom, she wouldn't hear any of this with the sound of running water so near, this was something that only Toby and Dean knew about and it wasn't making Toby very happy, he could feel he could cry at any second but he'd be damned if Dean would make him cry. Stare at Harold, thought Toby, just keeping staring at Harold and soon Dean will go away.

"Toby?" Asked Dean in a soft voice.
Toby looked up, blinking back tears.
"Are you going to cry baby?" He asked.
Toby shook his head, his bottom lip felt tight and wanted to move down at the corners.
"You can cry Tobes – he added mocking Jess's nickname for him – you can cry all day and every day in your little room. Princes often cry in their towers, but there is a new king in the castle now, I'm the new king and if you don't like it, you can fucking leave. There must be plenty of other carers who want a boy who cries when their sauce is taken away. Maybe you'd like me to talk to your mum about you going somewhere else to live. Shall I do that?" He stepped a little closer and snatched Harold.
Toby wanted to scream for his mum, he would have too if the taps had not stopped running, she would soon be here, she'll tell Dean off and make him say sorry and give Harold back.
"Ok Tobes it's, oh… Dean? Are you talking to Toby? Tell him his bath is ready" she walked away into her – technically, her and Dean's – bedroom.
"Yes, he's here, he's just showing me Howard, we're having a man to man chat about things" he added as sweet as a strawberry.
He turned to Toby, "we understand each other, don't we?"
Toby nodded and felt Harold hit his face.
"Here's your baby toy" Dean smirked and walked to find Jess.
Toby put Harold on his pillow and walked to the bathroom, in his mum's bedroom he could see Dean hugging her, Dean was two people, he'd heard about this from his mum, she had told him that sometimes people are something called two-faced, like the Batman character, one moment they can be your friend and seem to care for you and then the other, usually when you're not there, they can be cruel and say nasty things. Dean was horrible. Why didn't mum see this?
Before going into the bathroom, he dashed back to his bedroom and grabbed Harold, aside from feeling stronger with Harold around, it

wasn't safe for Harold to be left on his own, there was no knowing what Dean was capable of.

Toby stayed out of Dean's way as much as possible, it was not something he planned on doing but he instinctively gave Dean a wide berth and would invent reasons not to be in the same room as him. Summer was in full bloom and the garden gave Toby somewhere to spend time, no big sacrifice because he preferred the outdoors and wasn't like the other children at school who spent hours and hours sat in front of their televisions playing video games. That's all they spoke about at school, video games, who had completed what level, who had discovered what cheat and who was getting the newest game for the newest console, it was a full time subject between his friends at school and, because Toby wasn't really interested in it (and had nothing to bring to the conversations, that could last for days) he was excluded a little. No one wants to know that you can extract water from a cactus when you could design, build and master an entire world from your bedroom.

Toby became interested in the stars, he watched videos online about reading the different constellations and where they are in the sky, he became obsessed with the Northern Lights and was amazed to discover that you could see them from parts of Scotland. Scotland was another country but was far easier to reach than the northern countries of Scandinavia, they even spoke English. According to Jim, the Scottish were the best at making shortbread and they sold chocolate bars in fish and chip shops too, more things to make the idea of visiting Scotland more attractive. You could use the stars to understand where you were and in what direction to walk, you could make a line from the Big Dipper to the Little Dipper to find north, it was fascinating stuff. The television show he loved to watch was showing him how to do something called navigate, old sailors would use the stars to sail the correct way, maybe even the Vikings used it. The compass dad gave him was still tucked safely away beneath his pillow (he now put it in the pillow case so any curious people like Dean would struggle to find it) and it amazed Toby to think the little needle knew where the North Pole was, he understood it was something to do with magnets (magnets seemed amazing too) but what if it was so dark he couldn't see his compass? He would either have to wait until breakfast when the sun was up or use something else, the stars are always there, so he would one day learn how to navigate by the stars like a Viking.

Jess was at the school gates when Toby came out, she looked like she was unwell, Toby noticed it immediately, she was holding her arm and rubbing it through her coat. Toby thought she must be hot in the coat; it was not the warmest day ever, but it was still warm enough for him and the other children to be wearing shorts and polo shirts. Toby was showing her a drawing of a Viking long boat and explaining the shields on the sides when his mum interrupted him and told him that Dean was sad today. Dean had gone into work and was asked not to bother coming back anymore. This was confusing to Toby, people just went off to work and returned home later, he had not given any thought to where people went or if they might not be wanted there anymore. Toby looked blankly at his mum, his mind wandered between his Viking drawing and wondering why his mum was keeping her coat on. She must have a cold, he thought to himself, when he gets a cold, he is always told to keep warm. Before Dean invaded he would sit on the sofa and watch films with his mum if he was unwell, they'd drink orange juice and eat popcorn or lemon curd on toast, sometimes he would fall asleep to the sound of her breathing, her perfume mixed with the smell of her hair and the duvet that he would have over him. He would wake just as the end music would be playing and the Death Star had blown up, his mum would make an excuse like "I've seen that film so many times now, it makes me fall asleep" but he knew she liked spending time with him and she seemed happy fetching him drinks and food to keep him safe. It is a nice feeling being safe, he took it for granted and did not realise how much he missed it until just then. Dean had changed his home, it wasn't just the junk in his old bedroom, or the way his mums door was now locked at night, it was the small things like how Toby had to ask him if he wanted to go to the toilet or felt he had to rush to have a bath or shower. Dean was always saying things like "you eat too much" or "are you ever going to stop growing?" or "are you stupid or something?", it made Toby sad. It used to make him angry because dad never said these things, dad used to help him do things, he would help him read his books from school, he used to show him how to use the buttons with the letters on that was on the computer, he used to show him what a mouse did and he would let him dig holes in the garden and look under stones to find creepy crawlies. Toby was not wise, but he knew Dean was not as nice as his dad. These thoughts made him even sadder.

"Mum can we video call dad soon?" Toby asked looking at his mum.

"Hmm? – his mum replied – oh, yes, yes of course. We can do it this weekend if you like, I will send your dad a message and ask him if he's around. I know he'd love to hear from you." Jess smiled and ruffled Toby's hair.

She's not unwell after all he thought.

"When we get home, I want you to be extra good and be nice to Dean, he's worried about work."

"Why is he not allowed to go anymore?" Toby asked.

"Someone at work said Dean had stolen something and his boss found out, he's told Dean not to come back. He's lost his job." She explained.

"Can he get a new job?" Toby asked, if he was a brave child he would have added "somewhere a long way away, like the North pole or a space station?" but he wasn't brave and he knew such a comment would upset his mum and he didn't want to think about what would happen if his mum told Dean what he had said. At the moment life at home was just about ok, but Dean was like a see-saw, you didn't know which way he was tipping, sometimes he could be unkind and cruel and other times he would be like that Batman character again. His mum smiled and told him he could but the business he's in is very small, she told him it was a small world where everybody knew each other and it would take a little time before another job came up.

"Are you poorly?" Toby asked. His mum was sweating a little and she would not move her hand away from her arm, Toby was no doctor, but he knew if you were sweating it meant you were hot.

"If you take off the coat, you might feel better" he added.

Jess bent down and kissed him on the cheek, "what a clever boy you are, so considerate" she squeezed his hand and gave him a smile.

"I'm ok, just got a sore arm, I knocked it at work, I was putting things on a shelf and the box split and I was knocked"

Toby imagined his mum's arm was covered in sticky things like syrup or sugar or baked bean juice, if his arm was covered in that, he would wear a coat too to hide it. In this weather it will soon start to smell, it was better to keep food cool, otherwise it smelt which would attract rats and then snakes to the camp.

He really needed to watch less television.

Chapter six – The King Takes His Throne

Jess was right, Dean was in a foul mood when they arrived home, walking through the lounge, Toby saw a few empty beer cans on the table, Dean wasn't a big drinker but on the odd occasion he *did* drink, Toby kept far away. He was loud and stupid and it always ended up with his mum and Dean having an argument, a few times his mum had ended up crying and Dean would shout things like "I don't care who fucking hears" and "oh that's right, start fucking crying", Dean liked using the F word, occasionally he would use it towards Toby, but he never shouted it, he would come in close, so close that Toby would smell his warm breath and he would whisper it, it made Toby shiver.

"You'll do as you are fucking told" he would say.

This scared Toby. Toby had never really been scared before, there was a time when he was with his mum and dad and it was Christmas time, they'd gone into town to do some shopping and, when they were in a large shop, Toby couldn't find either of them. Everybody looked so big and it soon became a forest of legs, pushchairs and shopping trolleys, Toby quickly became upset, he remembered feeling panicked, everywhere he looked was a face he didn't recognise, even Harold was with his mum and dad so he had no one to help him. From out of nowhere he felt his dad's hands on his shoulders, it was a relief he had never felt before, it was soon forgotten but being scared was something that did not happen very often. He was not very good at being scared and he did not like it. Dean had the knack of scaring him and, what made things worse was, he seemed to like it.

Dean didn't look up when they returned home, Jess made her way into the kitchen, passing the table she bent and gave the tins a shake to check if they were empty and then gathered the empty ones to put into the bin. She steered Toby into the kitchen with her and bent low to speak quietly to him.

"Do you want to go into the garden and play Toby?"

Toby nodded and replied "you can come too if you want, I'll show you the whole in the ground where a fox lives" but his mum didn't want to come, he knew she liked foxes, even the ones that ran out in front of their car in the winter and made screaming noises at night. But she wanted to stay indoors and make the dinner. Toby felt bad for going into the garden, he felt like his mum was trying to get rid of him for a while, maybe she was going to tell Dean off for drinking, she didn't like him drinking in the daytime and as soon as the white tins of beer emerged from the fridge, his mum changed slightly. She stopped being smiley and happy and she grew unhappy, once upon a time she would have asked Dean to wait until Toby was in bed but, initially he would sulk and make some comment about Toby being some kind of spoilt prince so eventually his mum wouldn't say anything, she might give Dean a look or would breath out through her nose, just subtle things that only a son would notice but that had stopped too and slowly Dean was running the house. Maybe he was right when he told Toby a new King was in the castle.

Toby was playing at the top of the garden when his mum called him in for dinner, he stopped what he was doing and made his way down the path to the back door, Dean was nowhere to be seen. Much to the relief of Toby. His mum seemed much more relaxed and dinner was calm and friendly for a change, a little like the old times when his dad had been gone a few months and life was finding a new groove and routine.

"Has Dean gone to find a new job?" Toby asked while he was cutting up his omelette.

"No." His mum replied. It was a cold no. A no that was made of thick, solid granite with a layer of dense ice around it. It was the kind that was unmovable and unlikely to change, there was no point in discussing it any further, there was no knowing where Dean would be and no chance of his mum telling him, the case was closed.

"How big is a fox hole?" Toby said changing the subject.

"Oh, I don't know, I don't think I've ever seen one. They must be pretty big for the fox to be able to fit down."

Toby chased a piece of egg around the plate, the hole at the top of the garden was not very big, maybe it was a hole for a rat, or a snake. For some reason both animals brought Dean to his mind, Dean was a snake, *and* he was a rat.

Later that evening, Toby was playing in the bath, he loved pouring some water from one cup to another and making more and more bubbles, his mum could do whatever she wanted while he was doing that and she took the opportunity to wash his hair, wash behind his ears and she often sang a song to herself. How simpler life was when it was just the two of them, it was a much nicer house, Toby understood that his mum wasn't going to be on her own forever, his dad had told him that during a video call a few weeks ago.

"Your mum is a good woman, she won't be on the shelf for long" he had said, Toby understood the shelf metaphor, and he agreed that his mum was nice, but he didn't understand grown-ups at all, if his dad thought his mum was so nice and someone would be lucky to have her, why did he leave? It didn't make sense. Celia was nice too of course, but mum was mum, she was different. He was often told that good people get good things and bad people get bad things, that's why he should always be nice to people and good at school, and, so far, that seemed to be working for him, but what did he do to deserve Dean and, more to the point, what terrible thing did mum do?

Toby could see the top of his mum's arm and noticed a bruise there; it was big, purple and was shaped a little like a square but went almost all the way around the top of her arm like some kind of strange bangle or awful tattoo.

"What's that?" Toby asked pointing at the top of his mum's arm.

It looked very painful, he had had bruises before but none as bad as that, this bruise was something his mum would have described as angry. Angry normally meant it would take a few days to go and it probably hurt if it was touched.

"It's nothing to worry about, I told you earlier that I hurt it at work." She carried on washing his hair and got his towel ready, just then the front door opened, and they could hear Dean entering the house.

"Dean's home" Toby said sullenly. Peace was over he thought to himself.

He noticed his mum go tense and she paused slightly on hearing the door slam closed.

His mum was scared, Toby knew how she felt, he was scared too, he didn't know why, perhaps Dean is feeling happier now, if Toby is fed up he often goes outside, his mum says that people go for a walk if they feel unhappy or have difficult choices to make, it clears the head and allows people to think straight. But from the look on his mum's face, she was not convinced which made Toby think that too.

"Jess?!" called Dean.

"I'm up here, - she called down, and then, to Toby added – Toby go into your room and get dressed. I'll see what Dean wants."

"But what about supper? Shall I come down and..."

"No – Jess cut him off sharply – go to your room and get dressed, I'll come up and see you soon".

She left the room and Toby did as he was told. There was a time to not listen and this wasn't one of them, Toby went to his room and could hear Dean talking to his mum, he sounded different, he wasn't as clear as he usually was, his voice was a little slower and he repeated himself a few times. Toby knew this meant he was drunk. He knew people used to act strange if they had drunk too much wine, he'd seen it at Cath's birthday party last summer, Jim was a little different and his mum told him he was something called tipsy. Another person called it 'jolly' and it was ok because Jim was a nice man, and he was just celebrating his wife's birthday. Jolly did sound nice, and Jim seemed a little friendlier, but Dean did not sound friendlier, he sounded weird. If Toby wasn't so frightened, he would have probably laughed at the way Dean sounded but no one laughed at Dean. Particularly Toby.

Toby was dressed and into bed, he could hear his mum and Dean downstairs, mum had put the kettle on and was trying to get Dean to drink some coffee, but Dean was saying strange things. He was complaining that he was hungry and wanted something to eat, he started swearing and saying there was never any food in the house, that he was so hungry and he was angry at mum for not leaving him some food.

"I bet you two had something to eat" he called out.

He heard his mum talk, but she was much quieter, all he could make out was some noises that was her talking but the words were too quiet.

"Yeah I bet, you give him everything he wants, spoilt little shit, he's probably upstairs listening now" he added.

His mum said something about it being impossible for Toby to ignore it given that he was drunk and shouting, she said it was a good job Jim and Cath both had bad hearing or else they'd be knocking on the walls. Dean said he would knock Jim *through* the F-wording wall.

This went on for a few minutes, Dean saying something stupid and his mum arguing back, before long they were both shouting, and Toby grabbed Harold and sat on his bed away from his door. He missed his life before Dean came, he missed life before his dad left and he wished the shouting would stop and his mum would come to bed, away from that monster downstairs.

George at school had said that his mum and dad used to fight every night, they used to argue about anything, and the walls would shake with the sound of slamming doors and raised voices. Was this what was about to happen? Was this the future Toby had to look forward to? How did two people go from loving each other to fighting and hating each other? It was too much for Toby to understand.

Suddenly, the shouting changed direction, Dean had left the kitchen and was in the lounge, he could hear the sound of a crisp packet and thought Dean was eating crisps. His mum was still in the kitchen because he could hear her putting cups away and opening and closing the fridge, she was probably making him some supper or her lunch for the next day at work. She usually took a sandwich or something to eat, she said it saved money by not using the canteen at work, but she also told him on Friday's she would treat herself to a cream cake, it seems you never grow out of liking cream cakes.

After a while his mum came to say goodnight to him, he gave her the biggest hug he ever had, his mum was his hero and she stood toe to toe with that monster downstairs until Dean gave up and left the room, in Toby's eyes she was David versus Goliath, the small, brave warrior against the lumbering oaf. She took some shots but fired back better ones until the coward retreated with a bag of crisps and his tail between his legs. No doubt in the morning, Dean will feel stupid and apologise to his mum and Toby for the way he behaved. If Toby had come home drunk and was shouting at his mum, he'd be made to apologise a hundred times over, he'd go next door and say sorry to Jim and Cath and, if he was in, the chap who lived next door that worked for the circus as a clown and was always travelling the country having buckets of glitter thrown over him. Mum was brilliant but she did not stand for rudeness.

Toby dreamed about his dad that night. He was walking through the forest, he was wearing mustard coloured socks and carrying a backpack with his computer resting on the top and black wires trailing behind him. Toby and his mum were walking nearby, chatting to Celia about trees, animals and living in Canada. Toby had to watch where he put his feet because there was boggy mud all around them and one bad step could mean your shoe would get stuck and you would have to carry on in just your socks. Toby felt his backpack grow heavier and heavier, and it was difficult to keep up with his mum and Celia who would not stop talking and did not notice he had dropped back with every step. He could hear a noise in the trees and a black bear came walking out, his fur was splattered with bits of white, his growl sounded strange and he moved like he was one step from falling over. He looked at Toby and licked his lips, he was not scary, Toby wasn't frightened, but he knew he had to reach his mum and Celia, there was safety in numbers. He knew not to climb a tree because bears are expert climbers and it would follow him up, he tried to call out to his mum but she couldn't hear him, Celia was talking non-stop and his dad was striding ahead looking at the horizon and glancing at his compass.
The bear was too close now and would no doubt reach him. His dad suddenly appeared out of nowhere and pushed the bear over, he fell

into the dirt with a whumph and covered his face with his big paws. Toby stepped towards his dad and felt his shoe come off in the mud. He looked down at his yellow shoe, the shoelaces like bunny ears being the only things visible. Then he was awake.
Hungry.
The room was dark, and the world was silent, it was obviously very late (or very early, depending on how you looked at this sort of thing) and would be ages until breakfast. His mum didn't bring supper and he wasn't allowed to keep food in his room; besides, Harold would eat the biscuits and any crisps. He would be brave and go downstairs.

Downstairs was just as dark, there was a light coming from underneath the door to the lounge, Dean must have forgotten to turn it off when he went to bed, but it illuminated a part of the hallway carpet so Toby was able to see a little more. On entering the kitchen, Toby saw two cold cups of coffee and one of the chairs pulled away from the table, it looked like neither his mum nor Dean drank the drink his mum was making for them.
It felt strange being downstairs at night, it was like he was a burglar or he was in a shop after the last customer had gone, the room was silent when usually there was the noise from the washing machine or radio or the voices of him and his mum. It was somehow eery and he felt like a stranger, a trespasser breaking all the rules. He made up his mind to keep very quiet and to grab a biscuit and go back to bed, he had school in the morning and was forever being told how important sleep was and how much he needed.
He took the packet of custard creams from the cupboard and took one out, one would be enough, he would have preferred to have it with a cup of tea, but he wasn't about to wake his mum up and he would never wake up Dean to make him one.
He had put the packet back into the cupboard, closed the cupboard door and took his biscuit, suddenly he was off the ground being spun backwards by someone. He noticed the biscuit fly under the kitchen table, and it grew smaller and smaller and he was dragged from the kitchen and back into the hallway.

"So, you're a thief as well eh?" Dean hissed.
Toby landed on his back with a dull thud, it made his back hurt, and his breath was forced from his body. He saw something dark being tossed past him, it landed against the wall and fell onto Toby's legs, it was a suitcase, Toby winced and looked to his side, Dean had opened the cupboard beneath the stairs.
"Not a fucking sound" Dean growled.
Toby was wide-eyed and open-mouthed, his heart was slamming against his chest and he wanted to get up and run away screaming for his mum, for his dad, for Jim next door. He only wanted a biscuit, he was hungry, his mum said she would come and see him when he got ready for bed, why was Dean looking under the stairs? That was where dad went before he left, was Dean leaving? Was Dean going and he was telling Toby not to tell his mum so he could go without saying goodbye?
And then it dawned on Toby.
This was Toby's new room.
Toby watched in confused bewilderment as the door was pushed closed and he had to pull his leg away before the door slammed against it, where was mum? Why wasn't she fighting for him?
Toby was so scared, he could not stop his heart beating fast, he couldn't calm down and he couldn't stop the tears pouring down his face. His trousers were wet from where he'd wet himself, mum wouldn't be very happy about that, he hadn't done that in years, even when he was playing with his friends and he'd forgotten to go to the toilet, he still made it just in time. It was dark and frightening, the only sound was his crying and he knew Dean hated to hear Toby cry, he had to stop, he had to stop now, what if Dean was out there listening at the door?
Toby, sniffing back snot and tears, tried to stop the sudden jolts that were travelling through his body, he reached forward slowly and felt for the door, he pushed, but the door was locked. He was stuck.
He then heard footsteps on the stairs directly above him, Dean was going upstairs. He heard the bedroom door open and Dean shouting something, his mum screamed and something that sounded like a

clap rang out. Toby clasped his hands over his ears, his mum was in trouble now, he did not want to hear it, he was of no use down here in the dark, afraid and defeated. The king had claimed the castle and now he was using his power against Toby and his mum. No matter how hard he pressed his hands against his ears, he could still hear his mum crying and pleading with Dean to stop.
Eventually, Dean did stop. But the crying didn't.

At some point Toby understood that someone had left the house, he had heard footsteps passing the cupboard and the front door was opened and closed. He had no conscious thought if it was Dean or his mum, if he had he would have prayed and hoped that it was Dean leaving and not his mum. Did she even know he was down here? If not had she gone to his room only to find it empty and had rushed out into the night to find him? Thankfully, Toby was too exhausted to have these thoughts, he was in a deep but uncomfortable sleep.
Time had passed and he was woken by someone coming down the stairs very slowly and gently, it was his mum, he could hear her murmuring something and what sounded like crying, but ever so gently.
She went into the kitchen and she heard her move out a wooden chair and sit down. The chair groaned across the floor and she must have been moving because she suddenly came out of the kitchen and called up the stairs for him.
"Toby?" she called from the foot of the stairs.
She was a few feet from where he was, but he wasn't sure if it was safe to come out.
She called again and started walking up the stairs, Toby hit the cupboard door and called out "Mum, I'm in here".
Jess stopped on the fourth step and ran back down, she unclipped the small lock on the door and opened it, her face was one of shock, her expression totally confused as she reached in for him and placed her hands under his arms and pulled him out.
"Oh my God, oh my God" she said over and over, "what happened, what did he do to you?" She looked him up and down and, noticing

the dark patch around his crotch, realised Toby had been under the stairs for some time, maybe all night.

"I'm sorry mum" Toby couldn't help but burst into tears, tears of relief, fear and shame.

"My poor boy, I'm so sorry, I'm so sorry" she was squeezing him tighter than she ever had before as if she could squeeze the pain away.

Toby started telling her what had happened, how he woke up hungry and wanted something to eat but did not want to wake her up. How he came downstairs and wanted to take a custard cream, how he knew he shouldn't have more than one, how he was careful to put the packet back so they wouldn't go soft and how he was picked up by Dean and put under the stairs. He couldn't finish his story without crying and he apologised for wetting himself.

His mum did not care, she was crying too and shaking her head. It was then that Toby noticed his mum had a dark red line running down her bottom lip and pink grazes on her forehead just above her eye.

"Did you fall out of bed?" Toby asked. He'd seen these types of marks before, he had some of his own a little while ago when he fell off his scooter or when he ran too fast past a brick wall and his elbow rubbed the stone, it grazed his skin and was sore for days. A part of his mind told him that Dean had done this, these marks were not from falling out of bed, these happened when someone hit someone. One of his classmates used to come into school with marks like these, his name was Tom. Tom used to be very quiet if you asked him what he'd done, the teachers acted differently around him and after school, when the parents would come and meet the children, the other children's mums wouldn't stand near Tom's dad. Even Toby's mum would frown at Tom's dad.

Tom is much happier now, Tom's dad isn't allowed to see Tom anymore, he missed a few weeks of school and then he was back, he used to visit Mrs. Aseef, who was something called a counsellor, Tom visited her twice a week at school and he said that they sat and talked about things.

Dean had hit his mum.
This was the saddest Toby had ever felt.
His mum was too clever to realise that she couldn't lie to Toby, this wasn't the time for lies, instead she told him that Dean was angry last night and he lashed out at her, but she was fine, bruises heal and Dean had gone.
Hopefully, that would be the end of him.

Chapter Seven – To Reclaim the Throne

Things returned to normal for a little while, Jess did not go to work, she told her boss that she had come down with some virus and needed some time off to get better. She rarely took a sick day and was told to get better and not to rush back.

Toby got his video call with his dad and he was given the added responsibility of being allowed to make the call himself, normally his mum would do it, have a quick chat to Brian and then leave Toby and his dad to catch up before returning to finish the call correctly, but this time was different. When his dad answered Toby was beaming with a proud smile. His mum gave him strict instructions not to say anything about Dean, he was not to tell him that Dean had lashed out and definitely not to say anything about being put under the stairs. She said it would only make his dad worry and, besides, Dean was gone now. She would tell Dean to come and collect his things from the spare room, once that happened, that would be the end of it.

Toby wanted to tell him about how horrible Dean was, how he had thrown him in the cupboard and how dark and scary it was but he knew it was serious and his mum was always to be trusted in these situations (although, up until a few days ago, this situation hadn't actually existed), so he promised he would say nothing.

This secrecy extended to all members of the family and even to Jim and Cath, Toby was to say nothing to anybody. One day, whilst Toby was playing in the garden, Jim asked him how his mum was because he had not seen her for a few days.

"She's fine, she's a little bit poorly, but she's fine" said Toby.

"Well give her my love, being unwell is awful" Jim said.

Jim was laying out tools on the lawn and kept disappearing into the shed and re-emerging with other strange objects. He had trowels, bags of soil, a fork, spade, string, a piece of green sponge that he would kneel on and trays of different flowers. He must have walked back and forwards four or five times before he settled down to work. It made the conversation very difficult.

"What are you doing?" Toby asked, eying the different things Jim had to carry.
"Bedding up - Jim replied – I've had these plants in the greenhouse all spring but it's time for them to come outside and get put into the ground".
"Looks like hard work" Toby offered. He preferred to make holes and fill them with leaves and dirt, his mum called him the Sludge Prince, it had been a while since he had done it, Dean used to make comments about it, maybe he'd make an effort to do some this afternoon. Mum wasn't in a rush to go outside yet so he could make the biggest, deepest hole ever.
"It's not hard work if you enjoy it" Jim said smiling.
"You won't be saying that tonight, once you're all stiff and feeling ancient" Cath had appeared carrying a blunt piece of wood that he knew they referred to as a 'dibber'. It had made Toby laugh when he first heard the word.
"How's your mum Toby? I haven't seen her in days" Cathy handed the 'dibber' to Jim and looked back towards Toby.
"She's ok."
"She's not very well, Toby says she's poorly." Jim added, he gave Cath a look that Toby hadn't seen before, it was a little like the look the teachers gave when someone said something a little unbelievable.
"Oh, that is a shame, and how is Dean? We haven't seen him either, have we Jim?"
Cath knew, Toby thought, Cath knew. He had read books about old women having magical powers, they could read your mind and steal your thoughts, but Cath wasn't like the old women in the books, she didn't have a cat or a pointy hat.
"I don't know" Toby answered. It was not lying, he truthfully did not know, he had not seen Dean since… well, since that night, for all Toby cared Dean was at the bottom of a cliff or under a big rock.
"Do you like Dean?" Asked Cath.
"Cath!" Jim piped up.

"What? Jim it's fine, we're just talking aren't we Toby?" Toby nodded, but was feeling a little uncomfortable, maybe digging the hole would have to wait, he wanted to go indoors, it did not feel right deceiving people, especially people he liked.

"I like my dad more. Dad was much nicer." Toby said, he had not realised but he was looking at the floor, a woodlouse walked past and climbed down into a small crack in the broken, hard grey soil. Jim looked at Cath, who was looking sadly at Toby.

"Do you think I've got all the tools I need Toby?" Jim said brightly. Toby looked up and looked at the tools around Jim's feet, "I think so, you seem to have a lot".

"He should use his cart" Cath said, giving Jim a pretend look of fury. "It would save your knees, using the cart".

"Cart?" Toby brightened.

"Yes, I've got a cart for the garden, it's handy when I need to move something from the car, or if I'm lugging soil or sand around the place. Want to see it?"

"Yes please." This was amazing news, there was a cart right next door and Toby had never seen it.

Jim turned and went into the shed and came out carrying a rectangle of black metal with four wheels in the middle of it facing inwards.

"It folds up, so it takes up less space in the shed – Jim explained inspecting the cart – but if I lay it down and pull this arm…"

He put it on the floor and pulled up an 'L' shaped piece of metal with a sponge grip.

"… it becomes a cart."

The cart was red canvas with black nylon trim stretched across a black tubular metal frame. There were some pockets at the front near the extended arm that you used to pull it. The four wheels were at each corner, the front two steered and there was even a brake that would lock a wheel if the handle was twisted.

Toby thought it was the most amazing thing he had ever seen.

"The wheels are solid rubber, so they don't get punctured by thorns or sharp wire, it's a brilliant thing, I just don't use it enough." Jim said.

"No, you don't, you speak about it like it's a classic car, as if it's too nice to use." Cath said.

"I think it's brilliant!" Toby added.

"Well, if you like it, why not pop over and have a closer look, you could put the tools in it for me if you like. I'm not getting any younger."

Toby did not need to be asked a second time, he almost feel over the low garden fence in his haste to get to it.

He stood back from the cart to truly take it in, he could fit in the cart no problem (he'd been in smaller spaces recently) and, although he would need to bend his legs, he could easily lay down in it.

"Is there a roof too?" Toby asked as he moved the cart backwards and forewords slightly.

"No, no roof, it's made for moving things not going to the seaside in" Jim chuckled. He could see Cath smiling too.

"How do you keep the things dry then?" wondered Toby.

"Ooh, I don't know, I suppose you just wouldn't use it in the rain" Jim said.

"You could put a big umbrella over it. One of those big golfing umbrellas." Cath suggested.

"I guess you could if you could find one. Mind you'd have to keep it from blowing away."

"You could tie some weight to the handle, a big brick or something." Cath was full of great ideas. It was her, a few months ago, who decided to add Maltesers to her chocolate brownies, that was a great idea, Toby ate his at school with his friends looking on with envy. It was also her that showed him how to make paper chains for the Halloween party, and of course it was her idea for Jim to have a cart.

"I'd love a cart like this" Toby said wishing it were nearly Christmas.

"Well I do let my good friends use it occasionally" Jim teased, looking at Cath.

"Really? I could use it?" Toby jumped.

"Well I don't know, are we good friends?"

"Yeah!"

"In that case, I suppose I *have* to let you use it" Toby gave Jim a hug and thanked him, he said he would use it to move things around the garden and he wouldn't break it.

Cath and Jim smiled at each other, Toby was such a nice boy, they both thought, they were lucky to have such nice neighbours and, if the noises they heard a few nights back was anything to go by, Jess was lucky to have that horrible Dean out of her life.

Jess returned to work and Toby busied himself between school and being a seven-year-old, he occasionally used the cart to walk around the garden, he would pretend he was delivering letters and parcels to the different corners. One day he was a postman, the next he was a doctor delivering brains to hospitals and one day (and this was a story he returned to over and over) he was an explorer like the man on the television and he was travelling down the Amazon, or over mountains or through rainforests. He had to find water because he only had enough for a few days. The cart was somewhere Toby could imagine a much larger world, he would find new animals, new people from long-forgotten tribes and he'd hide underneath the cart when danger came, animals or warriors from the tribes would never see him because, when Toby instructed it, the cart became invisible. Jess told him that Dean was coming around to pick up his things from the spare room, she instructed him to stay outside and keep out of the way. Toby was happy to do that, if he never saw Dean again that would be just fine.

He heard the door knock and, as agreed, his mum asked him to go into the garden. He did not have Jim's cart that day, so he sat at the top of the garden and, half obscured by the hedge, peered through a gap in the foliage and looked out for danger.

He could see his mum making Dean a drink, they were talking and Dean was looking down and shaking his head, he looked so sad and was saying something to his mum that made his mum angry and then she looked like she was telling him off and then she hugged him. What? Why is she hugging him? Dean took the drink from the kitchen top and they walked into the lounge. Toby could not see much more from where he was, but he wasn't worried, his mum had put Dean in his place and Dean was probably trying to go. His mum was good at making you feel sorry for doing something, she was more than a match for that idiot.

After a little while, Jess came into the garden and called Toby over.
"It's ok, Dean's gone" she said giving Toby a hug.
"Has he taken his things?" Toby asked.
"Yes, some of them, there was too much for him to take in one go so he'll need to come back again and get more"
"He didn't look very happy."
"He wasn't, he was very sad and said he was sorry for what he did."
Toby just looked at his mum, he was not interested what Dean thought or felt, he had hurt him and his mum and the sooner he was forgotten about, the better.

Of course, I could end the story here, maybe I could add an epilogue involving Toby growing up without any lasting damage and living a full and happy life with a wife, children and a Jack Russell called Terence. They could all live in a nice street away from the hustle bustle of a city, they all might own matching wellington boots and spend the weekends exploring woods and clumps, eating sausage rolls and laughing from dawn until dusk. Life would be fantastic, an everlasting cocktail of laughter and white wine spritzers.

Maybe Jess went on to meet someone and her life too was enriched with the effects that love can bring. She would look back on her time with Dean as a stupid mistake, a chapter to be remembered but always thought of with caution and a constant reminder to her lucky escape and resulting better life. Brian and Celia ran a software training company in Vancouver and would visit Toby as often as they could, they would hand pick clients so they could come to England, Toby would bring his family to Canada as often as time and money would allow and all members of his extended family would spend Christmases together.

What a lovely, tied-with-a-bow finale for this tale, but things are rarely so neat and tidy, and rarely do bad things simply go away, and Dean, well he did not go away.

Scientists will argue that evolution is such a slow-moving phenomenon that it is almost impossible to see, slight changes take thousands of years to fully find their place, but Dean worked much faster. Using his junk in the spare room as a kind of anchor, it enabled Dean to stay in contact with Jess, his half-hearted promises of hiring a van and picking it all up came to nothing and four months later, he was doing something that Jim described as courting Jess once again.
"He must have a silver tongue that one" Toby once heard Cath say to Jim.
Toby knew what she meant, it did not take a genius to work out that Jess was once again falling for the charms, and attention of Dean. He had told them both that he had got another job, he was no longer drinking and was ashamed of how he had behaved, he blamed the drink but, his argument was, as he was no longer drinking, a repeat simply wouldn't happen again. And, he added, if anything did, Toby or his mum were welcome to call the police and have him taken away.
To Jess's credit, she did not take his word as gospel, she was cautious and ensured things moved slowly, she needed something that she called evidence before allowing Dean to come back in. Toby tried to make sense of this when he saw Dean's work clothes on the washing line. It felt like things were not only moving quickly but also backwards.
Jess had made Dean a meal one evening and she had asked Toby to go to bed to give her some time with him, Toby was happy to, he didn't want to be around Dean any more than absolutely necessary so he agreed and he toddled off to his bedroom as Dean came through the front door.
Dean gave Jess a kiss and, on seeing Toby walking up the stairs, said hello.

Toby replied "hi" but did not turn around or stop walking, he wanted Dean to know he did not want him there and he wasn't welcome. Maybe his mum had forgotten the tears and the bruises, but Toby had not, and it would be a long time before he did.

Toby could hear his mum and Dean talking downstairs, the clatter of cutlery against crockery, the sound of glasses being refilled, it sounded like it should, no raised voices or accusations, maybe his mum was happier when she was with Dean, it was obvious that she needed the attention he gave her and Toby couldn't expect his mum to wait around for his dad to come home forever. Jim had said something about his mum holding a candle, but from what Toby knew, the only candles they had were ones for birthday cakes and the white one in the downstairs toilet that smells like washing and is never lit because it was a gift from Jess's mum. If it was not to be used, why keep it in the toilet?

Toby struggled to sleep that night, he insisted on having a plastic mug of water and a biscuit by his bed now, so he never had to get up in the night. Going to the toilet was different, you could not ignore or avoid that but going downstairs for something to eat was something he did not want to do for a long time.

For some reason he awoke when he heard his mum downstairs, the room was dark, and he had been asleep for only a few hours. Dean must have gone already, he was not allowed to sleep over, not yet anyway, his mum had made that clear, her search for evidence was serious and she always stuck to her guns on these decisions.

He made his way downstairs and saw the kitchen light was on, the lounge lamp was on too and the tv was switched on very low, he could see his mum's jumper over the arm of the chair.

"Has Dean gone?" Toby called out, his voice was low, so not to wake anybody, who he was going to wake was anybody's guess but habits are habits.

He walked into the kitchen, he could sense his mum behind the door, probably putting something in the fridge.

"No. I'm still here." Dean said.

Toby went cold with fear, it was a strange feeling that felt like water running through his veins, dropping his body temperature and raising his heart rate in a split second. What the hell was Dean doing here, and where was his mum?

Toby instinctively looked at the cupboard under the stairs, was she in there? Would she even fit in there? He urged himself to think straight, to not panic, to not make any sudden moves, the man on the television told him that sudden moves make predators strike in the wild, they hunt by sight and are alerted by sudden twitches. The main thing is to keep calm and back away. So, he did.

"Where are you going?" Dean asked, his voice full of menace.

"Back to bed. I, um, I"

"It's nice that you've stopped being rude, I said hello to you earlier and you walked away, even had your back to me." Dean interrupted.

"I had to go to bed. My mum told me." Toby said, that was true too.

"Didn't mind having an early night?" Dean was dressed in a tee shirt and shorts; he had made a drink for himself and was putting the milk back when Toby had come in. Toby cursed himself for leaving his room, but he had already decided if Dean put him anywhere near that cupboard again, he would scream and kick until the walls of the house cracked and fell. He was ready to make the world shake; his mum would wake up and it would all be over for Dean.

"Sometimes I'm allowed to stay up but not tonight. Mum lets me watch television and we stay up later." Toby was proud when he said this, his mum was great, he loved her completely. He wished she were here right now.

"You can watch tv with me if you want? I'm only watching a film - Dean bent down to be closer to Toby – I won't tell your mum." He added.

"No. I should get back to bed, I'm going to be tired tomorrow."

Dean would not have it, he put his hand behind Toby and led him into the lounge, Toby grew cold again as he felt Deans hands pressing against his back and pushing him out of the kitchen.

The television was quietly showing adverts, Toby knew he shouldn't be seeing them, they were different from the ones he saw, instead of adverts of pet food, kitchen cleaner and groceries it was late night phone lines, adverts for betting companies and things like blenders and juicers being shown. None of it really made sense.

"You'll like this programme, it's an old film, but still really good." Dean sat Toby down in front of him, Toby was sat between Deans legs, his thighs pressing against his hips with Deans forearm around his waist.

It was a film in a shopping centre, lots of people were walking around the shops like they were drunk, stumbling into things and groaning, they all had pale, blue skin and it looked strange. There was shouting and fighting and people had guns but when they shot the people with the blue skin, nothing happened, they didn't fall down like in Star Wars, they kept walking and then, if they found one of the shouting people, they would eat them. This frightened Toby and he tried to look away but, if Dean saw, he would grip Toby's face and force him to watch and said things like "you wanted to stay up late you little shit" or "enjoying the show?".

Toby wriggled forwards and stumbled onto the carpet, Dean stood up and pushed Toby down, Toby skidded across the carpet on his knees and felt heat and sizzling pain. His hands slapped the floor and they ached.

"Go to bed!" Dean hissed in Toby's ear.

Toby jumped up, his lips trembled, and his breathing was fast, but he was not going to let Dean see him cry.

He sprinted up the stairs and ran into his room, he slid across the bed (more pain to his knees) and buried himself deep into the folds of the duvet and waited for morning.

A few weeks later, once Dean had fully moved back, Dean told Jess that they ate far too much tomato ketchup, "we spend a fortune on the stuff" he argued. He added that it wasn't cheap and only one person in the house had it anyway. Jess told him that a bottle of ketchup was not going to break the bank and Dean let it go, but he gave Toby a dirty look, Toby felt himself shrink into the kitchen chair.

Dinner time felt like walking across a rickety bridge, one false step and you would fall a hundred feet, you had to pick your words carefully and remain happy towards Jess but respectful and wary towards Dean. This was a dangerous animal that Toby was sitting across from, one not to be riled or teased. He had no sense of humour and no patience for his girlfriend's son. Toby had wanted to tell his mum about Dean making him watch a scary film, he'd wanted to say so badly but he knew she would tell him that she would speak to Dean about it which would only make Dean deny it and then Toby would face whatever punishment Dean would dream up. The only places Toby felt safe were school, his bedroom, Jim and Cath's garden and his own. Dean never went to the top of the garden where the fence was so low that Jim and Cath could speak to you. Jim and Cath would see through the disguise that Dean had in place, Cath did not like Dean, she would never say it, but Toby knew. Sometimes you just know something without any proof, it's like a sixth sense, a little like the way Toby knew someone was behind the kitchen door, it's just a shame he didn't have a seventh sense so he knew *who* it was.

Toby video called his dad at the weekend, it was great to see his face, Celia was there too, sitting right beside him and Toby thought his dad sounded a little different, Celia said that he'd spent too much time around some of her friends and that he'd picked up a little accent. To Toby it sounded like his dad was becoming American, but Celia said there was a big difference between American and Canadian, she even went as far as to say English people sounded Australian to her. Australia was miles away from England, Toby didn't think you could get any further away, but Celia was so nice that Toby let it go, he just smiled and asked if dad knew when he could come and visit.

"It's funny you say that Tobes – his dad said – is your mum nearby? We've got something to tell you both."

Toby called his mum and Jess came and crouched down near Toby.

"Hi Jess, we've got a bit of news" Brian said.

"We're engaged!" both Brian and Celia said at the same time.

Celia put her left hand up to the camera and Jess saw the sparkly ring on her third finger. Jess was surprised by how she felt, there was no jealousy or anger or upset, she was genuinely happy for her ex-husband and his partner, it was clear that they were both happy and Jess was happy with Dean. Of course, things weren't quite the same as before, before he did the thing she never dared think about or dwell on – and God knows she told nobody about, even Toby had no idea what had happened that night – but she smiled back and said congratulations.

Toby was a little different, he was pleased for his dad and his mum seemed happy so there was no reason not to feel happy but after a second or two he wondered what this meant for him, where did he fit into his dads life now that Celia would soon become his wife. Jess gave him a big kiss on his cheek and said, "that's from you Brian, I know you'd want to kiss Toby". She looked at her ex-husband and saw that their lives were changing, their lives were expanding and a small part of her longed-for Dean to put a ring on her finger. But she quickly shook that thought away, what nonsense she told herself, as if her and Dean were in the same place as Brian and Celia, but, in time, that thought led to the inevitable question; if her and Dean weren't in the same place as her ex, what was the point?

Dean was standing just outside the door, just within earshot while all of this was going on, his head was experiencing a mixed feeling of anger and jealousy, he had no idea why, he didn't even wonder why, he was an angry and jealous man. He could only concentrate on listening to the woman he slept with being happy for her ex-husband. What an odd way for someone to act, she was obviously still in love with her ex, he would never be able to replace him or make her feel that way about him. Then there was the child, he idolised his dad, even though he left them and moved across the world to live with the woman he screwed behind their backs, he would never look at Dean like that. The little shit was rude and ignorant to Dean, he never once realised how much work it took for Dean to keep this act up, if it wasn't for the fact that Jess was a sexy piece of ass, he wouldn't bother with the kid, he was an annoying fact, a bystander in this, like a punctured tyre on a classic car, he was a stain on the relationship and made Dean's life infinitely more difficult. He stopped them going to pubs, going on weekend breaks, Christ he even stopped Dean having friends over, kids sleep through noise, they practically go into a coma once they are asleep, a nuclear blast wouldn't wake them.

Dean stopped eavesdropping and went into the lounge and put on the television, he tried to think about other things but he couldn't stop thinking about why his world was so difficult and why was he constantly battling against it?

Chapter Eight – Children in Africa

Working in a supermarket had its perks, Jess was entitled to a small reduction in her shopping bill, it wasn't even ten percent but over the course of a year it meant she was saving money that could be put away for Christmas or perhaps a trip to Canada. If Brian and Celia decided to get married sooner rather than later, she would need to come up with the money for two tickets quickly.

Two tickets?

Wouldn't she need three tickets?

Surely, she would invite Dean too.

Dean was living with her, sleeping in the same bed, helping to pay the bills and they were living like a married couple. Toby had adjusted to the new arrangements better than she had hoped, she had noticed he was spending more and more time in his room but she thought this was natural, he would get bored of being with her and Dean and, being an only child meant he was used to being alone. These early months of summer had him out in the garden more than usual, his relationship with Jim next door was lovely to watch, Jim was a lovely man and you could see he enjoyed spending time with Toby as much as Toby did, plus he was a willing helper around the garden and Jim wasn't getting any younger. Cath was a retired school teacher so she could handle children as well as anybody, they didn't have any children or grandchildren of their own so maybe this suited them perfectly, a child that visited but also didn't stick around too long to become a nuisance.

Yes, she would need three tickets, Brian should have met Dean before, but there was a still a level of shame in Jess's mind. It was hard to make sense of it, but there was nagging doubt that still plagued her feelings for Dean. Brian never made her feel that way, through dating, planning a life together, the trying for a child, the cost and emotional toil of IVF and the disappointment when the cost simply outweighed the moral question, he was a solid pillar she could count on, quietly stoic and dependable, well that was until, as her mum had put it, his head was turned.

Brian always swore nothing had happened between he and Celia, it was a relationship borne out of conversations and a connection rather than cheap hotels and sordid meetings behind her back. He had never lied to her before and she knew he hadn't started for this, but it still hurt, it had made her feel like the world had ended, their little life, their little family split open like a coconut, with sharp edges and the feeling that it could never be mended. But they had worked hard at remaining civil. Jess took a level of comfort in the fact that she was not cheated on, that Brian hadn't used their bed to seduce Celia, it was done neatly and with respect, and there was Toby to think about. Toby adored his dad, he still does and longs for the next video call or one of the hand written letters Brian sends to him every few weeks, Toby keeps them in an old Clarks shoe box in the bottom of a drawer, they're stored in order of delivery and Jess is allowed every so often to read one. They're beautiful things, each one carefully considered and written, not once is Toby made to feel anything other than loved by his dad, it's heart-breaking to read because Jess knows Brian misses Toby as much as Toby misses Brian but geography can't be argued with. Jess doesn't have a skill that she can transfer to any part of the world, arranging who works in what part of a shop isn't in the same bracket as software design, or as well paid, so in England she remains, cut off from her family in the North. But her life down South is ok, she has some friends, she has good neighbours, and she has a terrific son who is growing up with a sense of intelligence and consideration, and she has Dean. The rough diamond, total opposite to Brian, maybe that's the reason she is sticking with Dean, her relationship with Brian seemed perfect and it failed, maybe with Dean, it'll work.

.

Jess is struggling with her bags of shopping, they clatter her legs as she shifts her weight from one to the other as she walks, Toby is trotting ahead with boxes of cereal and multi packs of crisps, light but bulky and awkward to carry. He puts the key into the front door, and they enter.

Dean is sitting on a chair in the lounge watching sport on the television, Jess gives him a look and says "it's ok, we've got it" as she struggles through the hall into the kitchen.
"I've been at work since seven!" he barks back.
Toby puts the cereal on the table and goes out into the garden.
"Hang on Usain Bolt, you can wait a minute, let's put this away first, Dean doesn't seem like he's about to rush to help"
Toby turns and comes back in; he starts taking items from the bags and passing them to his mum.
"I've been working woman!" Dean shouts.
Jess shrugs and takes things from Toby.
Dean struts into the kitchen and eyeing the ketchup glares at Toby.
"Ketchup? Back to that are we?" he says to Jess.
"Yep, Toby bought it himself, with his pocket money." She gives Toby a wink.
"I'm giving him pocket money, now am I?" said Dean
"No – Jess turned to Dean - I am."
"There are kids in Africa with nothing to eat and here he is buying luxuries like tomato ketchup!"
"It's not exactly a luxury is it? A luxury is something like lobster or caviar." Jess continues to move about the kitchen, putting things in the correct place.
Dean walks out of the room and Jess smiles at Toby.

That evening Toby was busy reading a book that his teacher had asked the whole class to read, it was about a young girl with a pet pig, Toby quite liked it but he knew he was behind in his reading. Reading wasn't something Toby particularly enjoyed, it didn't come natural to him, his mum had told him that once he found a book he liked, he'll discover how lucky he was that he could read and a whole new world was waiting for him. Jess told him he could have his dinner in his room if it meant he kept reading, Toby thought this was a great compromise, he was happy to read because not only did it break one of the rules of the home; no food in the bedrooms, but it also meant more time away from Dean.

As promised, his mum came up the stairs with a plate of potato wedges and a hot dog in a bun for Toby, there was a second sausage on the plate in case one was not enough. Toby pretended to be fully engrossed in the book as his mum put his plate down, in truth he was only half interested in the story, he wanted to read books about brave explorers discovering waterfalls and battling giant snakes, not a girl with a pig and a clever spider.

Just as Jess left Toby noticed she had forgotten the ketchup. They bought some that very day, so he knew it was not because they had run out.

He called after his mum, who, by now was halfway down the stairs.

"Ok – she replied – I'll fetch you some but keep reading" she called back.

A few seconds passed and he could hear here back on the stairs, he buried his nose back into the book and started crunching on a potato wedge. Dean walked in shaking the ketchup bottle and clicking off the lid.

"Where do you want it Your Highness?" he said.

Toby looked up, his guard immediately risen, "Just on the plate please, I'll dip it in. Thank you."

It was always a good idea to remember one's manners when faced with a monster, just on the off chance they were still deciding whether to eat you or merely sniff you and leave.

Dean bent down so the bottle was a few inches from the plate and started to squeeze the bottle, the sauce came out in a lush, thick stream.

"Say when" Dean said.

Immediately Toby said "when", but Dean didn't stop, the sauce still came out.

"Say when Toby" Dean said again as the puddle of sauce got larger and larger.

"When!" Toby said a little louder.

Still Dean carried on, the sauce was taking over the plate, there was far too much to eat and Dean was wasting it.

"When. When! Stop!" Toby called.

"Ok, ok, - Dean said stopping – no need to shout, I'm not deaf" Dean was smiling, no doubt aware that Jess may have heard her son calling.
"Is everything ok?" Jess called up.
"Yes, it's fine, Toby was so busy reading he forgot to say when, he's got a bit too much sauce now" Dean called back as sweet and as cute as a doting parent.
"I wouldn't bet against him eating it anyway." Jess called walking back to the kitchen.
Dean turned to Toby who was busy staring at the mess on his plate, Toby was frowning at the sauce, he wanted to call Dean a monster, but he also wanted to cry and run to his mum. Toby did nothing, he sat and waited, pleading for Dean to leave his room, to leave his house and his life.
"Your mum wants that plate clean Toby" Dean said looking down at the sad seven-year-old.
"Ok" Toby said almost silently.
"Oh, and Toby?" Toby looked up.
"Don't make a mess" Dean squirted the bottle in Toby's face, it went on his chin, his mouth and dripped down his top, it made Toby jump and his book fell onto the floor, as he looked down at it, he saw a red splodge on the cover.
Not blood, he thought, not blood, just sauce.
Dean walked away saying something under his breath and trotted down the stairs.
Toby could hear his mum say something to Dean as he re-entered the kitchen, Dean replied "yeah, he's fine, he's having a party up there".

For the next few weeks dinnertimes became unbearable and frightening for Toby, his mum would ask almost every day if anything was wrong, a mothers instinct is truly powerful but it can't read minds and it can't solve mysteries like why a son has begun to eat a fraction of what he used to. Could it be his age? Was he becoming aware of food and diet? It was something his school was hot on, childhood obesity was becoming more and more widespread and dangerous, children preferring to stay indoors glued to consoles, tablets and televisions instead of climbing trees and running through streams. Perhaps Toby had taken the dietary advice too seriously but he was in no risk of being obese, he was a slim child, active and fit, a summer of fetching and carrying things in Jim's garden took care of that. Yes, his favourite food was anything ketchup-flavoured, but they rarely ate takeaways and would never sit in front of the television with chocolate or popcorn. Jess understood the importance of health and she was raising Toby to understand it too. Did Toby act differently around Dean? It was difficult to know for sure, Toby was normally at school and he was rarely left alone with him, if that was a subconscious decision or not, Jess did not leave Dean and Toby alone very much. Dean was not a natural father figure, he did what he did and if a child fitted in, great, if not, well Dean was not about to change his ways to fit in. This suited Jess fine, secretly she loved having a special place in Toby's life and, with Brian gone, her role became even more crucial.

If she thought about it she would have noticed that she herself was eating less, she put it down to the change in the season, she would often eat less as the warmer weeks of the British summer took hold, out went the cottage pies and heavy roast dinners and in came the salads, barbeques and dinners that borrowed heavily from the Mediterranean ingredients of cous-cous, fish and fresh tomatoes. Fruit was always available at home and, again only realising when she came to do the weekly shop, she was buying more fruit because her and Toby was eating more of it. Dean didn't change his diet, he was meat and veg all the way, when he wanted steak, he would go to the pub, see some friends and order steak. When he wanted lasagne; he went to the pub for that too.

I would dare say that if she stopped and thought about it (like she would at a later date) she would connect the dots between her eating less and her listening to Dean's barbs about her weight and the amount her and her son ate. The old saying of 'sticks and stones...' is partly true, sticks and stones break bones, but the bit about words is only half true, words do hurt, but in a slower - but ultimately - more permanent way. What starts out as a silly joke can develop into something much meaner until every mealtime is a lesson in subtle abuse and hatred. Dean didn't complain about how Jess looked when he was in bed with her, he would often say how good it felt to be inside her (a thought Jess didn't very much like, she saw sex as a coming together, a display of love not simply putting part A into socket B) and sex was becoming increasingly routine. Hardly ever was Dean gentle or patient, if he wanted sex he would man handle her until she gave in, her periods weren't allowed to get in the way, they were annoying and he would swear blind that they happened more regularly than once a month, he would grow impatient and demand sex, if she wasn't forthcoming he would sulk and make her feel dirty or ugly. He would comment how she would gain weight during her period and nature's way of preventing this was to have sex. Sex was exercise after all.

"You're really enjoying your dinner tonight, aren't you?" was how it all started.

It was a subtle seed that found a nurturing place in Jess's mind, over time it grew and grew.

"Do all women eat as much as you?" was another.

"How many calories should a woman eat per day?"

They all hit their intended target, to question, to create doubt, to hurt, to ultimately make you feel uncomfortable and worthless.

Jess saw Toby eat less and she too ate less. But, secretly, they were both hungry.

Jess would eat at work, the cream cake on a Friday was gone, no longer did she eat the treats but co-workers noticed and complimented her, after all to lose weight is seen as a badge of triumph, something to celebrate, but Jess was never overweight and would never be for the remainder of her life.

Toby could eat at school, he often had school dinners, but he was like his mum, not greedy and only ate what he needed to play and function as a child.

They had both lost weight. Jess's family thought too much.

Eventually the video calls to her mum ceased, all they would say was how much weight the pair was losing, were they ill? Was she struggling for money? Did she need a better paid job? They were welcome to move back up North where the daily diet was bread, kebab and pies, that would get the meat back on their bones in no time.
Jess grew tired of deflecting the questions of concern, it was all they ever asked about, so she started using the phone instead, it is easier to say you're fine when they can't see you.

Toby started looking too thin, his teachers had asked Jess if everything were ok at home, they could help with paying for her son's school meals if money was tight at home. Jess was offended by such a question, she prided herself on her ability to juggle motherhood and her working schedule.
"Things are fine" she told Mr. Andrews, she said it was the change in the weather, they didn't cook large meals but things would return come the colder days, and they shouldn't jump to conclusions based around somebody eating healthily, there were children in the school with bigger problems than these made-up ones, maybe they should switch their attention to those children.
But Toby was shrinking, his clothes no longer fitted correctly. Being a tall boy meant he wore clothes for older children anyway so now his clothes looked baggy and unfitting. The parents at the school gates noticed, soon rumours and questions about his health came into question. Parents are often ignorant and wild comments come into play, this one's daughter said this and this one's son heard someone talking to someone else and apparently Toby has got a rare condition that stops him gaining weight, pretty quickly those rumours grow into fact. Add to that the never-ending stream of bruises that Toby seems to have.
This was put down to Toby's health too.
It made complete sense to the other parents that when a child is undernourished, they are weaker, they might lose balance easier and would inevitably fall more regularly. When Toby wore shorts, the

bruises were difficult to miss, but they were in the typical places that young boys have bruises, on the knees and the elbows. He must have fallen off his scooter, the poor lad.

But other parents have a habit of being caring and concerned until they are away from the school gates, once that happens, its forgotten. They might say something about that child from school who is obviously unwell, they may even remark how there is a child in their son's class who has recently lost weight and comes to school with bruises on his knees but they don't join the dots.

The truth (and it is a dark truth) is, Dean was not only influencing how much Toby ate, but he also had a hand in how Toby was getting these bruises. Dean had found enjoyment in pushing Toby, so much so that it had become a regular thing, you see without knowing it every bad thing that happened to Dean during the course of his day was Toby's fault.

Someone made a joke at Dean's expense. Toby immediately came to Deans mind.

Dean lost a game of pool at the pub. That was Toby's fault.

Toby may have been three or four miles away, but he somehow had shifted Dean's luck, so Dean experienced bad things. Dean would go home plotting and fantasising about hurting Toby. Oh, how he would love to throw him from the bedroom window, how long would it take for Toby to reach the path below? He would wonder what shape Toby would make on the hard floor, would he land face down or on his back, would there be a lot of blood and if so, how far would it reach before it stopped seeping from his little head?

Dean's mind could become a cruel, dark, vicious, poisonous place. Thoughts best left in a counsellor's office or prison cell. He found himself brightening as he walked home, he would promise himself rewards for not hurting Toby or Jess, maybe he would fuck Jess just that little bit harder tonight, why not, she liked the feeling of him inside her, she liked to moan, to be on the edge where pleasure blurs into pain. He had wanted to bite her before, to bite her ear as he fucked her but when he bit her shoulder, she did not shut up about it for weeks. Who cared that it bruised, he certainly did not, it was just

a playful nip, to see if she liked it? He convinced himself that she was going to pay for it tonight, he would get that little shit to bed and then show Jess what he was all about. She was lucky to have him, he told himself, she was saving money, looking better than she ever had – but she was looking like she'd lost weight, he wasn't sure he liked that, she was losing weight around her bum, which he didn't want to happen and for some reason, her breath sometimes smelt.
By the time his mind had run through these thoughts he was home, and he was determined tonight was for him to have some fun.

Toby awoke in the cupboard again. His neck was sore and one of his knees was bleeding, there was a dried line of blood running from the wound over his calf and it hurt when he picked at it. The cupboard was pitch black, this was becoming more and difficult, for some reason it was becoming less frightening, but he could not get used to the dark.
He had started to go to bed with a pin in his pyjamas so he could slide the pin through the gap in the door and lift the little latch that keeps the door shut. The latch was shaped like a question mark but sat loosely in an 'O' shaped ring.
His most recent video call to his dad was cut short after Dean had been glaring at him, video calls had become rare and now he had to use the phone to speak to his dad. He still received letters but even these were getting fewer, he wondered if someone was stopping him seeing them.
He had asked his dad for a torch and his dad said he'd send one if he wanted but he was better off getting one in Britain, the big shop near him would have a good selection, they might even have grown up ones that are waterproof and you can throw from an aeroplane and they still work. Toby did not want one of those, but he also wanted one that would not need new batteries all the time like some of his toys that he used to play with.
"You can get wind up ones Tobe" his dad said.
"What are wind up ones?" Toby asked.

His dad then described them to him, they sounded perfect, they did not have a battery that needed changing, they used something called a dynamo that charged the light, so it shone. Toby could put it in the cupboard under the stairs and use it whenever Dean decided to put him in there.

Toby had once heard that lots of little changes eventually add up to make a big change. Perhaps it was time for some small changes.

Chapter Nine – Big Shop

A short walk from Brook Gardens was a huge mega supermarket, it was open from very early in the morning and didn't close again until way after Toby was in bed, it was larger than two football pitches, so large in fact that Toby always stayed close to his mum if they ever went there.

His dad was right, they would have torches and Toby could easily go and buy one. All he needed was money and a way to cross the busy roads.

The money part was relatively easy, he received money from family members on birthdays and at Christmas and, if his mum hadn't yet paid it into the bank, it should be in a drawer in the kitchen. He couldn't remember having bought anything big recently (to Toby, big things were more expensive than small things, in his mind a balloon costed far more than a diamond ring) so there could well be millions of pounds in the drawer. The trick was getting in there without being seen or raising suspicion.

He'd seen television shows that when things needed to be gotten without people knowing something called a distraction was made. These usually involved a lot of noise or someone dropping a bag of shopping on the floor so people were busy helping picking it all up. He knew he needed to make Dean and his mum to look the other way so that weekend, just after his mum was putting the breakfast things away, Toby stood near the drawer and looked into the garden.

"Is that cat having a poo?" he asked to nobody in particular.

Both Dean and his mum looked out of the window, both scanning the area for the offending cat.

Toby opened the drawer and saw a little plastic bag with some ten-pound notes folded inside, that was it, he recognised the bag, that was what he was after, but Deans hand landed on his and it squeezed. Tightly.

"Oh, sorry Tobes – Dean said innocently – I didn't see your hand there" Toby pulled his hand away and the drawer slammed shut. Toby looked at Dean and left the room.

"What was that about?" Jess asked Dean, Toby didn't hear Dean's response, no doubt it was a lie, something his mum would believe yet again. Toby was out the front door and in the front garden.
He would have to think of something else.

Opportunities come along in life more often than you realise, the deciding factor is whether or not you recognise them and take them. His second chance came the following weekend, his weight was continuing to fall slowly and his stomach would regularly let him know it needed more food. He wasn't able to run around with his friends as much at school, he would grow tired quickly and need to sit down, but he told nobody what was going on at home. It was a lonely existence but one he was determined to change.
Jess was reluctant to leave Toby under the care of Jemma, she hadn't had anybody babysit Toby in such a long time and she didn't really want to go out, but Dean was persuasive and he had been given tickets from a mate at the pub for an outdoor showing of one of Jess's favourite films.
The film was about to start at six, it was being held at a large private house with nicely landscaped grounds and afterwards there was a bar and a few of Deans friends were intending to go. For Jess not to go would be a mistake, he would hold it against her for months and she had had enough of fighting. It was obvious that it was better to keep your mouth shut and do as you were told.
Jemma had visibly changed, to Toby she looked like a grown up and dressed like the pop stars on the television with two or three different colours in her hair, a loose tee shirt and mobile phone glued to a pierced ear.
Jess and Dean left a little after Toby had something to eat and Jemma was told she was welcome to a snack and a drink, Toby had some reading to do but he should be in bed no later than eight o'clock.
As soon as the front door was closed Toby played out his plan.

It was nice seeing Jemma again, and Toby felt bad that he had to deceive her but, if everything went to plan, she wouldn't know anything about it and no one would get into trouble.

Toby allowed Jemma to get settled, she generally enjoyed watching films with Toby, it was an easy way to earn money for a teenager with a fondness for new clothes. She was too busy counting and spending the money in her head to argue with Toby when he said he was quickly approaching eight years old and that it came with responsibility (his dad had told him that in a recent conversation, "Toby, you're getting older now, you'll soon be eight years old and you need to be more responsible, just little things like getting yourself dressed and not having to be asked to go to bed, would go a long way to helping your mum out" he had said) so he told her he would do some reading and then get himself ready for bed. He went as far as to say he loved reading so much that he would often do it until he couldn't keep his eyes open. If Jemma saw him again this evening he would be surprised because he just went off to bed on his own.

Jemma's eyes lit up, she could text her boyfriend and look at the sales on her phone, this evening was getting better and better.

Toby went off to the kitchen to get his money from the drawer, "are you ok Toby?" Jemma called from the lounge, the television was already on and he could hear little bleeps as she received messages.

"Just getting a drink first" he said.

He opened the drawer and, no money.

The bag was there, but it was empty.

Dean, thought Toby.

Toby closed the drawer defeated. He looked around the kitchen, could he swap something for a torch, could be sell something and spend the money on a torch? He looked at the hooks on the wall where his mum put the spare keys for the front door, back door and the spare car keys and then he saw it, a small, circular piece of metal that was attached to a key ring.

"Shopping trolleys" he said to himself.

Suddenly he wasn't a defeated seven-year-old, he was devising a new plan.

He went into the lounge, said goodnight to Jemma and went upstairs, Jemma was too distracted by her boyfriends inexperienced attempts at seduction to wonder why Toby was carrying his trainers, for all she knew he walked up the stairs and went into his room. She then heard his door open and close; he was happily in his room reading his book. He was a nice boy, probably the nicest boy she looked after, he was certainly the politest and he was very bright. He seemed to have lost a little weight but children grew quickly and his tummy was probably trying to keep up with his bones. His mum was nice too, she'd also lost weight come to think of it (and teenage girls notice these things) but she was always friendly. But the boyfriend was a strange one, she didn't care for him at all, she noticed him looking at her. He wasn't creepy or anything but there was something odd about him that she didn't like.
She was thinking this in-between her near-constant messages and didn't notice the seven-year-old return down the stairs and walk towards the front door, open it and walk out. No sound, no alarms. Toby sat on the front step just in case Jemma heard and came to investigate. After a few seconds nothing had happened, he heard her phone bleep once more so took that as a good time to put his shoes on.
He was out in the world and the only thing between him and the shop was some roads and the possibility of being seen by a concerned adult.
He stood.
He started to walk.
The late afternoon was lovely and warm, the sun was hitting his face as he took his first determined steps, this wasn't so bad he thought to himself, just don't look back and act natural (whatever natural was).
He made his way past the park where he and his parents used to play, he used to scuff his knees and trainers on the spongy rubber

matting that covered the floor, his dad used to push him on those swings and his mum would smear him in sun protection cream and force him to wear his hat and drink water.

He felt like a tourist to his own life, here he was striding confidently down memory lane, floods of thoughts and feelings flushed through his head and he grew sad by what he had remembered and what he had lost. But this was no time for reflection, there was a job to do, this was unchartered territory, had he truly believed his plan would work? Well it had and he was a step closer to the shop with every second that passed.

Turning the corner, he could make out the roof of the shop and the traffic suddenly became busier as more and more cars turned into the car park. Crossing the road was simple, he had to press the button and wait, he'd done this a hundred times before and was happy doing this part, he would wait for the green man and slowly make his way down to the shops, but before getting there he needed to check the trolleys.

A few years ago people had stolen trolleys, this was costing the supermarkets lots of money, they would end up in hedgerows and in ditches for miles around, Toby was told the story of how a group of teenagers got drunk at a house party and stole a trolley so they could push their drunk friend home. Everything was going fine until they got to the top of a hill and lost control, the trolley careered down the hill before slamming into the side of a road. The boy in the trolley was killed, squished like a pumpkin. So now you had to put a pound coin into a little slot to get a trolley, and sometimes people forgot their pound coin so Toby's plan was to check the trolleys for forgotten coins. He figured he needed eight to buy his torch so he couldn't go anywhere until he had eight pound coins.

It was a long job, there were so many trollies and the places people left them were a long way away from each other, it was a large area to cover and he soon grew tired.

He sat on a bench and waited for a man dressed in a yellow coat to bring a long line of trolley's back, there must have been hundreds of trolleys there, there was sure to be some money left. As he waited for the man to unhook a long strap from the front trolley someone put something in the bin to his left. He turned and noticed someone was throwing away some packaging from the burger restaurant nearby. It smelt good. He hadn't eaten a burger since his friend Sammy's birthday party late last year, he'd eaten cheese fingers rolled in bread crumbs, a burger, some fries and a cola, afterwards they had an ice cream and a toy and then the birthday cake and a party bag with a yo-yo and pencils and writing pad, he liked the food and tried to convince his mum to buy him it again later but she never did. She started saying something about how too many people eat it and it wasn't good for you but he knew lots of people that ate it and they seemed fine.

Finally, the man in the yellow moved away and Toby saw his chance, he walked to the trolleys and walked down the line pretending to count them, he said one, two, three... until he reached twenty-three and there it was, a battered one-pound coin. Toby's eyes grew wide he grabbed it and put it in his pocket.

One down, four... no, five to go.

No, one down, seven to go.

This might be easier than he thought. He set off to the furthest part of the car park, being careful not to make people suspicious, he had already had a few strange looks from people, old ladies were the worst, they would point at him and make their friends or husbands look over. Toby decided to walk close to a family so people would think he was with them and was lagging a little behind his brothers and sister, this worked well until he followed a black family, being white skinned he stood out and received even more strange looks, so gave up on that idea for a while.

Without knowing it he had followed his nose and had ended up near the burger place, there were one or two trolleys but they didn't hold any money. He was so far from the shop that it felt like a different world, the benches were different, the paint on the floor to separate the parking spaces were different and the bins were full of empty cardboard boxes and brown paper bags. Friday afternoon must be the busiest time of the week because the bins were full, but people still put their rubbish near the bins. Full bags of rubbish were being placed at the base of the bins. Toby was so hungry he felt like he could eat the aroma from the restaurant, the drive-through was busy with people queueing in their cars and people were walking in and coming out with bags of food. Perhaps this could be another answer to one of Toby's problems.

Toby watched a father get out of his car and carry the empty bag to the bin, he spent a few seconds looking for a gap to put the rubbish but he put it on the floor, as he returned to his car, his wife put down her car door window and motioned for him to take her rubbish, "have you finished that?" he asked her.

She nodded.

"You haven't eaten it" he said surprised.

She gestured something to him and he took it from her and put it in the bag he'd just put down.

Before he had returned to his car Toby was walking towards the bag, he didn't slow, he simply put his hand by his side, scooped up the bag and carried on walking.

By the time Toby had found a second, and third, pound coin he was sitting on a bench finishing his burger and the half a dozen fries that was left in the bag. He sipped a few gulps of cola and put the bag in the bin. As he was doing it, he looked up and noticed a man dressed in black. He'd seen policemen before but never this close and never one with a dog.

Toby liked animals and instinctively said hello to the dog.

He asked the policeman if he could stroke his dog.

"Of course you can, he likes the fuss. Well done for asking first, a lot of people just reach for her" he said smiling.

"It's a her?" Toby asked.

"Yes, she's named after the Queen, her name is Lizzie" he said watching Toby.

The policeman looked around the immediate area, no parents, no one looking out for this boy, he was too young to be out on his own, not a runaway, he was dressed too well to be living on the streets.

He was a little skinny maybe but he was eating, he was putting the rubbish from his dinner in the bin.
The policeman thought through different scenarios, who was this boy and what was he doing here were his first thoughts.
"Are you here on your own?" he asked.
Without skipping a beat Toby replied "no, my mum is inside getting cigarettes for my Grandad" he had no idea how he came up with such a lie, but he'd said it and couldn't take it back. The police wrote everything down in a black book so he couldn't change it.
"What's your name? Do you live near here?"
"My name is Toby and I live in Brooks Gardens, number 19, it has a blue door and a gnome in the front garden, we live next door to Jim and Cath, they're really nice." Toby answered as bright as a button.
The policeman crouched down and, immediately liking Toby, showed him how Lizzie liked to be tickled under her chin.
"She's lovely – Toby said – I'd love a pet dog but I don't think we can afford one, my mum works in a shop and I don't know who would walk her. Do you walk Lizzie?"
"I do but at the moment she's working, she helps me find things, things bad people don't want me to know they've got."
"Like guns?" Toby asked.
The policeman laughed, "well, hopefully not guns, I don't think Lizzie knows what a gun smells like, but she can find naughty things like drugs."
"Drugs? Wow" said Toby, he knew dogs had good noses but didn't know they could smell drugs, this dog was probably the best police dog around.
"You're so lucky to have a dog work with you".
"She's a good one, but I also work with another police officer, she's just coming now – Toby looked around and a second police officer was coming over – she's got me a coffee"
"Hello, and who's this?" the new arrival asked, she was a little shorter, had short blonde hair and her black vest made her look like she could solve any problem.

"This is Toby, his mum is inside so he's keeping me and Lizzie company"
The woman smiled and slightly frowned.
"Getting cigarettes" he added.
Toby stroked Lizzie once more and, noticing the men in yellow were bringing another delivery of trolleys over, said goodbye to the police.
"Nice to meet you Toby" the police officer said.
"Nice to meet you too, um, policeman" Toby added awkwardly.
"It's Craig, and this is Emma, you already know Lizzie" Craig finished.
Toby did his trick of pretending to count the trolleys, another coin found and as he watched Craig, Emma and Lizzie drive away he wondered if he would get into trouble for stealing food from bins or money from trolleys, he possibly could but if they knew why he was doing it, they might be gentle with him.
Toby was thinking about Jemma back at his home, was she looking for him? For all he knew she had gone upstairs to check on him, discovered he wasn't there and was at that very moment phoning his mum and Dean. His mum would be worried and Dean would be furious. He decided to go into the shop and see if he could find a torch.

The shop seemed much larger without his mum beside him, the ceiling was way above, so high that there were balloons tucked in the metal framework that were simply too high to recover with a ladder or one of those carts with the platform that beeps as they move. He'd seen these being used on the trees near his home, he often wondered how the world looked from up there, high above the pavement, looking down on the world and into bird's nests and bedroom windows. He'd seen people in bright vests change lightbulbs on the street lights, they would move and jostle a small stick in the platform that made the wheels below move. It looked fun. He wondered how long a balloon would stay trapped up in the roof before it slowly drifted down and whether you were allowed to keep it if you caught it.

He walked slowly through the shop, there were so many things to look at and buy, without his mum there he was welcome to visit aisle six, or as he knew it, the toy aisle, he could crouch on the floor and play with all manner of things, no one would hurry him up or tell him they needed to get going otherwise the shop will run out of food. This was his time, he could use it however he wanted but he imagined his mum getting the call from Jemma and telling a fuming Dean that she had to go home, he couldn't imagine the words Dean would be using but they would probably start with F and end with "ucking little shit", so he resisted the temptation of aisle six.

He needed an aisle that was opposite aisle six, he needed aisle thirty-nine, the electrical and lighting aisle, that was where the torches were.

The selection was impressive, there were torches with magnets, LED's, some shaped like ladybirds or bumblebees, some with bendy necks for looking into difficult to reach places and there were all kinds of sizes from ones for your keyring to large ones that were as large as shoeboxes that bragged a beam of light. Finally, he saw what he was after, it was green, simply made and had a foldable handle that tucked away into the body. It was perfect. He took one from the shelf and tried to read the little cardboard label that was attached, he didn't recognise most of the words but he could read 'Try Me' easily enough, so he followed the diagram that was on a sticker and turned the handle, a few seconds later he flicked the switch and a low yellow light appeared from the bulb. It worked. No battery, no fuss.

He then tried to find the price on the narrow strip of card at the front of the shelf, he had just the right money, he would even get five pence change (if his maths were correct). He felt for his money in his pocket and made his way to the checkout.

In a strange way, this was the most frightening part of his plan, leaving the house was simple, crossing the road was simple, finding enough money was something that would happen eventually, there are enough forgetful people in the world to get the money with enough time, but this was the crossroads between it working and failing. He decided to walk down the different checkouts first, he had to pick carefully, if he went to a person who was nosey, they would ask questions, and questions are difficult to answer. So he decided to avoid all women who looked like they had children of their own, then he decided to avoid men who looked like they might have children too, what he needed was someone that wouldn't ask questions, simply scan the torch, take the money and carry on working. It was obvious, he needed a teenage boy.

Friday afternoons are the busiest times for supermarkets, people are getting the shopping for the next week, maybe people have been paid and the urge to buy that extra bottle of wine or joint of pork comes into play, so the supermarkets want their best staff. Efficiency is everything in getting more people through the checkouts and more money into the tills, teenage boys were few and far between, they were stocking the fruit and vegetables not being trusted with credit cards and vouchers cut from magazines.

There was nothing for it, Toby had to bite the bullet and let fate get involved.

It was then that he saw Miss Kent, his teacher from a year ago, his first instinct was to hide but then something came to him, he'd go to the same checkout as her and, if possible, sneak in front to pay for his torch. There was nothing suspicious about a boy chatting to a young woman, especially when they knew each other's names, why it was the most natural thing in the world wasn't it?

"Hello Miss Kent" Toby piped up as proud as a peacock.

Miss Kent turned with a level of frustration, all she wanted to do was get her shopping, she'd spent all week being called Miss Kent and having countless high-pitched voices call her name. Her working week had ended, it was just her luck that she would get recognised and accosted while she was buying her weekly shopping.

"Hello Toby, nice to see you? Buying a torch eh?" her mask was fully restored, she could be Miss Kent for one more minute, and Toby was one of the nicer boys she knew.

"Yes, my mum is paying for the shopping over there – he gestured towards the other end of the shop, Miss Kent turned to look but Toby continued, drawing her attention back to him – she's trusting me to pay for this on my own, from my pocket money"
"Well I'm just about to pay for my things, but if you want to go first, I'll let you, otherwise you'll be here for ages and your mum won't thank me for that." Miss Kent was a good teacher and the children liked her (not as much as one of the caretakers at the school but that was another story - in a few months maybe he'll build up the courage to speak to her and maybe they'll find they have a few things in common and eventually he'll ask her for a date) but, until that time, she's content with her life of work, marking work in front of the television and wondering if one of the caretakers at the school was single because she rather fancied him.
"Oh, thank you" said Toby with a smile.
He put his torch onto the conveyor belt and, as he drew closer to the lady on the checkout, turned to Miss Kent and said "what's for dinner tonight?"
The lady on the checkout made the assumption we all would, this was a mother and son and, as usual, the son was hungry.
"Oh, um, I don't know yet, I'll think of something" Miss Kent replied. Toby nodded and could hear the beep of the scanner as his prize that was paid for with reclaimed money was logged into the system, elsewhere a piece of software informed the buyers for the shop to reorder wind-up torches, one had sold and a little boy now had the means to have some light when his mums abusive boyfriend decided he'd had enough of him. Toby gave the lady his money, she handed him a receipt and his five pence change and it was done.
He stood near Miss Kent's trolley for a second or two so to underline his rouse, thanked her for letting him push in and made his way out. He made a note to walk home via the bin near the restaurant and, as he approached, he stooped down, picked up a bag that was at the foot of the bin and carried on walking. By the time he reached his home he was in possession of a torch, one pound and five pence (he found another pound coin on his return journey) and was sipping the

last of a strawberry milkshake having put the remains of a burger and fries into another bin.

Maybe things were going to get slightly better from now on, because when he got back home and re-entered the house through the back door, Jemma hadn't moved, she was still texting on her phone and watching television.

He crept upstairs before turning and walking down again, announcing his impending arrival to his keeper.

"Everything ok Toby?" Jemma turned and asked.

"Hi, yes thanks, everything is fine" he replied.

He walked into the kitchen, took some sticky tape from the drawer and made his way to the under-stair's cupboard, opened the door and stuck his torch to the inside, just above the door frame, next to his pin for opening the latch.

He said goodnight to Jemma and reminded himself of what he had accomplished, he was resourceful and able and had a will power that he didn't know he possessed, he wondered what other things he was capable of as he walked up the stairs again and let out a burp that tasted of sweet strawberry milkshake.

Chapter Ten – Another Night in The Cupboard

Toby was able to watch some television, Jess understood that he loved watching the show about the adventurer who was taken by helicopter to a far-off land. At the start of the show he would jump from the chopper and make his way to a certain pickup point, negotiating certain dangers along the way. She had seen a few episodes but it all seemed over dramatized to her but she was happy for Toby to watch it, Toby had picked up certain nuggets of information that he used to share with her at mealtimes and it was better than him spending countless hours shooting aliens on a games console.

He could recognise different trees and knew which tree had fruit or nuts and which fruit you shouldn't eat. He knew the difference between horse chestnuts and sweet chestnuts, important knowledge if you wanted to eat one but was unsure which one was ok and which one would kill you. A few months ago, just after Dean had left, Toby had shown her how to make fire from putting a shoe lace around a stick and making something that looked like a violin bow to heat up another piece of wood before putting it on cotton wool and blowing it. He did it to heat up some water and making a drink he made with stinging nettles. She double checked with Google to make sure they weren't about to spend the night in A&E but it tasted fine, obviously it didn't rival a nice cup of Twinings, but it was ok and she could see the pride he felt for showing her his new skills. It was obvious he liked the outdoors and it made her wish that she had a larger garden with a treehouse for him to really let his imagination shine, but he was happy catching bugs and learning what they ate and where they lived, it was all information that was slowly building up a library of knowledge. Dean said he'd grow out of it eventually, and it was just a phase but Jess liked that her son enjoyed these things, it was what made him so interesting.

Dean had picked up some weekend work and he couldn't refuse the job; it was cash in hand so couldn't be turned down and he said he could do with the money to clear a few debts. Jess had no problem with this, it allowed her to spend some quality time with Toby and she made the most of it, they watched tv, chatted to Jim and Cath, took a walk to the park and did some cooking together, if she was more selfish she would have listened to her head when it told her this was how it used to be, this was how it should be. Dean was great of course but his bad points often outnumbered his good, actually, come to think of it, she found it more and more difficult to point out his good points. She often felt like this was simply a place for him to live where he got fed, got his washing done and, without sounding vulgar, got sex. The sex had quickly lost its appeal for her, she wanted to make love not make the bed squeak and she was constantly in a state of confusion because he would remark how she was eating too much at dinner time yet would complain that she was losing her shape, what was it that he wanted exactly? It's impossible to be both thin and fat at the same time. It secretly drove her mad and, inevitably she would draw comparisons to Brian, which was a bad thing, because next to Dean, Brian was a saint, but he was gone and you can't hold a torch forever. These thoughts returned all the time during the quiet moments when she was given time to think and dwell of things, it was a dangerous pastime because it always led to the same conclusion; they were happier without Dean.

"Your dad is calling today; I'll get dinner tidied away and you can have a chat" she said to Toby as he climbed the rope climbing frame, it made her nervous how he went higher and higher, but he was sure footed and had great trust in his grip strength.
"Will he ask me to be his best man?" Toby asked.
Children had a knack of plucking random questions out of thin air, without a warning you can be expected to know every tiny teeny piece of information, Jess hadn't even considered the ins and outs of the wedding. Brian had, for all intended purposes, said goodbye to his old life when he upped sticks and moved across the Atlantic, he wasn't exactly littered with friends anyway, his choice to work from home meant he had no work colleagues and he didn't keep in touch with University friends or people back up North, unless he's made

friends with the local Mountie, Toby could well be in with a chance of getting the job.
"I don't know, I hadn't thought of that, maybe." She said.

Upon arriving home, Dean was rummaging through the kitchen cupboards, he was clutching a piece of unbuttered bread in his hand and was still dressed in his work clothes. Toby's heart sank when he saw him, he felt his armour being applied and knew the weekend had come to an end.
Dean looked at them and continued to look for food, he grabbed a packet of crisps and walked past them, "I'm off to get tidied up" he grunted as he went.
Jess shrugged to Toby and made a glass of squash, Toby looked out into the garden, it had started to rain, he won't be able to escape today, he wouldn't be allowed to play in the garden and Jim wouldn't be out, he'd be tucked away in his shed or indoors with Cath reading the newspaper.
He was stuck inside. He'd have to keep out of the way until his dad called later.

Dean seemed irritable for the rest of the day, he would switch from loving partner to short-tempered in a second, leaving both Jess and Toby on egg shells, he was unpredictable but that was normally counteracted by giving him space and not giving him reason to escalate the problem but today he was different, he seemed to be picking an argument. Jess had recognised this early and was even more demure than usual, she sat with Toby in his room and helped him read through his story book. Toby was improving at his reading, the letters from his dad were helping because he wanted to read them himself and felt a great deal of accomplishment when he was able to read it alone. Brian was starting to use more and more words that he could read and would occasionally throw in a tricky one to get him using his sounds. Pretty soon Toby would be writing back to his dad and hopefully a long-lasting pen pal relationship might develop which of course would help his writing as well as his reading.

It was getting close to dinnertime, Toby would silently plea with his clock to slow down or stop, but time never does as it's asked, it just keeps moving and moving ever closer to the time when Toby must sit at the same table and feel the atmosphere clog the air like the tight pressure that occurs deep beneath the sea. It has the power to crush and makes breathing difficult. It's best to eat and run, but not too fast, if you eat too fast Dean would make you feel two inches tall, and you could only leave the table once he allowed you.

Jess left and went downstairs to the kitchen, Toby could hear her opening cupboards and preparing dinner, he could also hear Dean probing and teasing her about something or another. Toby hid Harold beneath his pillow again and went downstairs, he was afraid of Dean but he was also afraid to leave his mum alone, when it came to dealing with bullies, the more allies you had, the better.

Toby had never seen Dean hit his mum before and it was as if he was watching a film as he saw Dean push Jess against the wall and grab her face around her jaw. She looked so tiny pressed beneath Dean's male mass. Dean was considerably larger than Jess, he easily stood a head taller than her and had to bend down so his eyes were level with hers, he whispered something to her as he pressed closer and closer so they were centimetres apart, his hand pinching harder, fitting like a mask over the bottom of her face.

Toby felt an anger he hadn't felt before and shouted stop, he was amazed how his voice sounded and could hardly believe that sound came from his own mouth, it sounded so unlike him, like a scared boy, like an angry boy.

Dean turned in surprise at the small child, Jess turned her eyes at him and said something Toby couldn't make out.

Dean glared at Toby, it was a look that Toby never forgot, those fire-crazed eyes, that glare could turn a man to stone, but Toby stood stock still, not knowing it, but his face showed every ounce and molecule of fury that he felt towards Dean. It was a look that Toby should have disguised, maybe with a little quick thinking and rapid apologies he might have gotten out of it with a telling off, but it was too late, Dean had seen the revolt, there was a challenger to the throne.

Dean loosened his grip on Jess and moved towards Toby, almost stalking him, Jess pulled at Dean's arm and pleaded him to stop, to let it go, to forget it, to draw his attention back to her, she'd gladly take the punishment, if it meant being hit, so be it, bruises heal but not Toby, not her son, she looked at Toby and wanted him to run, he was fast and wiry, he could escape while she delayed Dean, but Toby couldn't move. Maybe part of him didn't want to.

Dean yanked his arm free, leaving Jess clutching thin air, Toby's feet finally sprung into life, the message had gotten through from his head and he started to move away, but Dean was tall and had long arms, he easily reached out and grabbed Toby.

He felt his arm pinch under Dean's tight grip and let out a small cry, his body wincing as he was pulled backwards. He heard Dean shout "get off" to Jess and he saw his mum being pushed backwards into the kitchen, she fell into the chairs and tumbled heavily onto the floor, Toby looked at Dean, he was furious, he could almost smell the smoke and the fire from the heat Dean was giving off. For some reason a thought crossed Toby's mind as he was being shook and pulled like a doll, he kept thinking about the red mist, he'd heard someone say it while he was forced to watch football with Dean one night, Dean had made him stay up late, waking him from his sleep and dragging him downstairs. One of the players kicked someone and the person describing the match said something called the red mist had descended, Toby couldn't see anything red but he understood it was something that suddenly took over and made people lash out. He could see red in Dean's face.

Dean screamed into Toby's eyes, his spit and breath landed on his skin making him cry, Toby didn't have the chance to put both feet on the floor at the same time, he was jostled and shifted from one side to another, never really gaining his balance and then he felt his hair being pulled, his head jerking backwards, he saw in a blur how his mother had got up, had limped to an upright position and was walking over, she started screaming something, it was loud and

primal, angry and demented, it was the saddest sound Toby had ever heard. Dean removed his hand from Toby's arm and, spinning in one motion, struck Toby's mum in the face, the silence was absolute, his mum tumbled and fell like a towel blown from the washing line in the wind. She hit the floor and didn't move.
Was she dead? Was she going to get up?
"Fucking stay there!" Dean said. So calm, Toby thought, he was calm. All fight was taken from Toby as he heard the cupboard door open, Toby instinctively turned towards the cupboard, better to go in than be thrown in he knew, but the adrenalin in Dean was too strong, Toby struck the back of the cupboard and crumpled to the floor, the door slammed closed and the latch was turned. It was a mixture of relief and worry as he laid there crying, listening to his breath and hoping his mum was still alive.

Toby risked winding his torch after a length of time, he had no idea how long he'd been in there, but he had smelt food being cooked, had heard Dean eat and throw the plate into the sink. The good news was the torch worked really well, Toby smiled a little as it illuminated the small cupboard space, he checked himself for wounds but aside from a bruise on his arm and probably a bruise on his back where he struck the wall, he was relatively ok.
He heard his mum talking ever so quietly, Dean was saying things back like "You can get up now, you useless bitch" and "clean yourself up, you're an embarrassment" and he seemed shocked when his mum said something to make him reply "nothing! He's in the cupboard, safe and sound".
Dean left the house and Jess scrambled across the floor to the cupboard, she reached in and pulled Toby out, her tears were getting heavier as she held him. She kept saying sorry over and over, she'd done nothing wrong, it was the monster, the King of the castle who had been horrible.
Toby shook as he cried and they stayed like that for a few minutes until Toby said "can I speak to dad now?"

Jess moved Toby so she could see him and shook her head, "I'll tell him we were invited out and can't make the call this week Tobes" and then apologised again.

The rest of the day was a time of quiet, Jess would suddenly and without warning start to cry as if she was reliving the whole experience, her face was swollen around her jaw and her mouth didn't move like usual because of the swelling but neither spoke very often. She made them something to eat, just some simple cheese on toast and she laughed when Toby said they should have this more often because he loves cheese on toast.

He went to bed clutching Harold and Jess went to bed soon afterwards, he heard her close the bedroom door.

He heard Dean come back a little later, the monster hadn't left for good then, he thought to himself in the dark.

Chapter Eleven – The Big, Wide World

One evening Toby was looking through old photographs, there were ones of his mum and dads wedding day, Jess had pointed to different people and explained who they were but he couldn't remember hardly any of them and the people he did know had changed so much since the photo was taken. Jess had said some of them had even died since then, it had been that long ago. He liked looking at pictures of his mum and dad when they were younger, it was funny to see them as his age, he wondered if they would have all been friends if they had gone to school together. His mum said she doubted it because Toby was a cool kid and she and Brian had always been geeky.

There were a few photos of him as a baby, but none with his mum and dad, his mum had explained how when he was born, he was taken from his mummy because she wasn't able to look after him. He couldn't remember his real mum; he was far too young. He had one photo of her but he rarely looked at it, it was just a woman that he didn't know, but Jess had told him to keep it safe because it was important to know where you had come from plus, someday, he might want to look at it and maybe find out a little more about her. He nodded and did as he was told but his life wasn't as interesting as his mum and dad's, they seemed to have had a life filled with holidays, parties, friends and strange haircuts (especially Jess who seemed to spend most of her teenage years changing the colour of her hair).

His mum had become quieter these last few days, her face had gone back to normal and Dean had done his usual thing of begging for forgiveness and trying to win her over with little signs of emotion and gifts. To her credit, his mum had put the gifts in the cupboard or took them to work to share with her colleagues, Toby figured she was too afraid of Dean to tell him to go away, he knew he couldn't do it and Dean might hurt them both again if she tried it.

The one good thing from all of this, if there was such a thing as a good thing, was he was able to move around without as much trouble, he was even allowed to go into the garden if it rained, as long as he was sensible with what he wore and didn't make a mess in the house when he came back in (which, he never did, he knew that meant more work for his mum and Dean being in a bad mood which was to be avoided at all costs). He even went as far as the big shop again and would sometimes search the trolleys for pound coins, he kept these under the stairs. The irony was totally lost on Toby, his secret hiding place was the one place he hated to be, but he also knew no one went in there, it had started to represent the day to day life at 19 Brook Gardens, the cupboard was dark, cold and uncomfortable and you felt cramped and confined in there, in much the same way that Jess and Toby felt every day.

He made regular visits to the bin near the burger restaurant too and his strength was returning, he often wanted to take something home for his mum but he realised this would lead to questions he didn't want to face just yet, he liked his journeys out and he liked the extra meals he was getting, he was starting to keep pace with his friends at school in the playground again. He was aware that his diet wasn't the best so he tried to eat as much as the salad as possible, he would often leave the bread and feast on the burger and lettuce, tomato and, having developed a taste for them, the slices of gherkin.

It was easier to leave the house when it rained, for some reason people seemed to choose that time to visit the shops and his bounty of pound coin and free food would go up. Jim said he liked the rain because nature did the watering for him, but Toby wasn't so sure. He'd once heard that there was no such thing as bad weather, just the wrong clothes and he liked that idea, the man on the television would say the rain brought different problems to overcome but at least you had something to drink. So, there were good things about bad things. On a return journey from the shops Toby, being four pounds richer and three hundred calories fuller, saw something sticking out from a black litterbin, it was an umbrella. It was unceremoniously dumped into the bin and Toby, having remembered what Cath had said about having an umbrella to keep the garden cart dry, raced to it and carefully pulled it out. He would show it to Jim and hopefully he can fix it. Toby didn't realise how significant this find was and how this simple thing would change his life forever.

As he grew closer to his home, he saw a familiar face walking across some grass and sniffing the ground, it was Lizzie the police dog. Close by, on the other end of the dog lead was Craig. He was stood looking very bored and saying something to his partner Emma who Toby could see sitting in the police car with the door open.

Craig saw him as he drew closer and said hello, "fancy seeing you here again, been out for a walk have you?" the police had a way of asking innocent questions that sounded like an interrogation, Toby was too young to realise this and simply replied yes and tried to hide the umbrella behind his back.

"Looks like your umbrella is broken, well done for taking it home, most people would throw it in the hedge or in the bin" Craig went on.

"Is Lizzie about to have a poo?" Toby asked strangely fascinated that other animals did what he used to consider funny. He'd seen dogs do it before and it often reminded him of the way ice cream came out of those machines in the vans that come once a day during the summer.

"She acted like she wanted to but I've been stood here for five minutes like a wally waiting for her to do something" he replied.

"It's more ten minutes Craig" Emma piped up from the car.

Toby looked towards Emma and said hello to her, he was many things but rude was not one of them. He was taught to say hello to anybody who said it to him and to never be rude; "manners cost nothing" his nan used to say. Brian's mum was his favourite of the grandparents, it was a shame he didn't get to see her as much anymore, he still received cards and gifts but he understood things changed once Brian went to Canada.

"Aah, here we go, throw me a bag Emma" Craig called as Lizzie started to crouch.

"Get it yourself, I'm not getting involved" Emma looked away.

Toby walked over to the police car and grabbed one of the bags he saw peeping out from the car door reservoir, he handed it to Craig and took a step back to play no further part. The actual act of seeing a dog poo is funny to most seven-year olds, but the smell certainly isn't.

"All done – Craig said tying the bag while Lizzie started kicking up grass – so do you live nearby then? I suppose you must do if you're out on your own." He looked at Toby and Toby nodded, he told him he lived at number 19 Brook Gardens. He went on to say he knew he was a little further than his mum would like him but she had started to let him go further from home as long as he didn't cross any roads or get into trouble. In fact Toby enjoyed telling people things about himself, he was an open book and it felt nice to talk to someone new, his life had started to feel very small and his world felt as if it was getting smaller and smaller, if it wasn't for his trips to the shops and the fast food place, he wouldn't travel outside of his house and garden for days.

Craig said he knew Brook Gardens, and he added that Toby was lucky to have such a trusting mum but she was right to be worried because the roads nearby were busy and there was never a shortage of trouble if someone wanted to find, or create, it.

Toby liked Craig, he seemed ok, he wasn't like the policemen he'd seen on television, they were either chasing robbers in cars or standing outside courts talking to people from the news, this one was much better, he had a radio on his shoulder and his own dog. Yes, you had to pick up its poo but that was a small price to pay for having a best friend and someone who would bark at bad men and, if you wanted it to, would bite the bad man so he'd run away and not hurt you again.

That appealed to Toby, maybe he could get a dog and teach him to bark at Dean if he started being nasty, but Toby worried that if he became too angry, he would tell the dog to bite or, better yet, *eat* Dean.

Craig and Emma liked having Toby around, most people looked the other way or acted suspicious around the police, there seemed to be a feeling of guilt no matter where they went, it was the same in their personal lives, Emma was married and had a plan to have two children by the time she was thirty, she'd like to buy a farm in Devon and be the local police officer settling disputes between farmers and maybe escorting a few drunks from the village pub or giving directions to the tourists that would litter the place come the summer season. But when she met new people they would visibly change when she told them her job.

"Ooh does this mean I should get rid of the stolen tv's in my garage?" they would joke, Emma had heard them all, "I better flush the coke down the toilet" or "I didn't do it, honestly officer" in mock protest, it was funny at first, she'd even found a level of pride in her job but her days were spent filling out paperwork, sitting in a car with Craig and his stinky dog and escorting drunks to the holding cells after being abused and spat at on a Friday or Saturday night. She struggled to keep her cool at times, how many more stupid seventeen-year olds does she have to plead with to go home or to stop stealing cars? Craig was a little older, he'd seen everything having spent time patrolling the motorways of Wiltshire for a few years and having worked at the border down in Dover, he'd heard every excuse and seen too many lives wasted on drugs, drink and poor choices. Lizzie was his way to find a little happiness in his work and he enjoyed the mundane jobs like stolen bikes, speeders and teenage gangs causing trouble in the town. He'd found having Lizzie allowed people to come closer and treat him like a person and not a man in a uniform, he would visit schools and discuss things with students of different ages. Trying to steer someone away from a life of illegal pursuits was better started young, he could recognise the trouble makers in an instant, these were often the ones at the back of the hall, the ones not listening, looking at him like some kind of enemy. There were those who liked the idea of the police, they would raise their hands, ask questions and genuinely seem intrigued by the life Craig had chosen. He would tell them stories about the Aston Martin that crashed into a concrete bridge at one hundred and twenty miles per hour, how the car was crumpled to such a size that the first responders took bets on what make and model the car was. The driver had died and, this is where he would turn serious, someone had the job of informing their family.

He would say that every action has a reaction and often those not involved were the ones that would end up being hurt the most, the mother of the daughter who died on her bicycle because of a drunk driver, the three year old girl knocked over at a zebra crossing in a hit and run. He would read the reaction of his audience and those at the back would giggle and snigger, these would be the ones he would be seeing in a few years once the routine of school had gone and they struggled to fill their hours.

Having the chance to talk to a little boy like Toby was a silver lining to their day, it was clear that he was bright, considerate and wouldn't be stupid enough to fall into a gang or succumb to peer pressure.

"We had better go Toby, it was lovely seeing you again, I think Lizzie enjoys having a new face around too" Craig knelt down and patted Toby on the shoulder.

"I reckon you could fix that umbrella – Emma said looking at it – I think it's just turned inside out from the wind" she held out her hand and Toby gave it to her, after a few seconds she straightened out one of the thin metal arms and opened it up.

"Good as new" she said proudly. Another problem fixed.

Toby waved goodbye and made his way back to his house, it was a few roads over but his mind was on the umbrella, he had a cover for the cart, he wondered if Jim would allow him to borrow the cart sometime, he could use it in the rain and maybe sit in it beneath the umbrella while it rained. He'd never done that before and he knew he'd enjoy watching the rain run down the sides while he sat inside as dry as a cactus in the sand.

Toby had put the umbrella under his bed and was looking at the photos again, so many things had happened before he had come along, it was one thing to imagine his mum and dad being young but then there was their mums and dads and then *their* mums and dads. He had been told a little about family trees at school, the teacher had a large poster showing the Royal family, there was the Queen near the bottom and beneath her were the people he saw on the television and on newspapers, and above her were rows and rows of people he had never heard of. His teacher had said some family trees were very interesting and you could look at parts of history and link it to who was on the throne at the time, they were lucky to live in a country where the history was so well documented and so much had happened. But Toby thought it sounded like lots of fighting, there was always fighting, England fought with France, they had fought with Scotland, then they fought with Ireland. The teacher said they even had a fight with America which sounded difficult when you think how far away America is, and then, when Britain fought Germany, America helped, this confused Toby, but the teacher said there was a few hundred years between. Toby had raised his hand and asked if Britain had ever had a fight with Canada, the teacher didn't think so but he then said, if not, they must have been one of the only ones.

It didn't make Toby feel very good knowing all Britain was famous for was fighting.

Toby found a few photos that he couldn't remember seeing before, it was a photo of some children and a baby, the baby was being cuddled by a blonde-haired girl, maybe that was his mum and the baby was his mum's brother or cousin. The little girl looked friendly and a part of Toby yearned for her, was this someone he knew too? Was it Cath from next door?

He decided to put this photo on the top of the pile of photos so he could ask his mum the next time he spent time with her alone. She seemed to be around less and less, was she unwell? She was tired in the evenings. Dean was still his usual self and had taken to drinking in the home now. There would be white beer cans in the bin, his mum would take them out and put them in the orange plastic bins they used to recycle certain things but she would do it without telling him or without him knowing. Dean would argue that when the binmen would collect the rubbish they threw it in the same truck anyway so how is that recycling, he thought it was something the

Prime Minister invented to make jobs for people and in fact it was a waste of time. He often thought and said things that Toby thought was the opposite of what he had been told. Toby's school had made a huge effort to recycle, he had seen programmes of the television about how there was so much plastic around that animals starting thinking it was food and started eating it, whales were eating bags, ducks were eating fishing line and dolphins were getting caught in nets. Someone told him that birds were eating the chewing gum that people spat out and choking on it, this was all caused by not putting things in the bin correctly. Dean would probably enjoy watching a horse drinking his beer and falling over, it was just something else to add to the ever-growing list of things Toby did not like about him.

Chapter Twelve – Heart of A Buffalo

Children seem to love looking at old photographs, the world seems strange to them, clothes look different, haircuts are different and those male members of the family that have turned bald all have hair, what a crazy window into the past a photograph is.

Who knows what it was that drew Toby to these photographs, perhaps it was the promise of a world much larger than the one he inhabited, maybe it was a form of escapism for him, a place to disappear to when his life became sad and lonely, but he would spend a few minutes each day looking at those photos. The one he returned to again and again was the one of the children with the baby, how happy they looked, each posing for the camera with a mood of closeness that only comes from a group of tight friends or family. The one thing that puzzled him was the different skin colours, they were certainly a mixed bag of people, but they looked happy and happy was something Toby hadn't been for a long time.

He finally got to see his dad via the computer screen that weekend, Brian had been messaging Jess every day for a date to call, he had missed his last chance and, if truth be known, he was getting worried about the irregularities in his contact with Toby, Celia had told him not to worry, the boy was growing up and would be wanting to be out with his friends or doing things that boys his age do but it didn't really put Brian's mind at rest. He started to wish he had kept in touch with those neighbours that were so friendly when he and Jess first moved in, he didn't want to spy on anybody, but it was reassuring knowing there were people nearby he could contact in an emergency.

Brian was proud of his relationship with Celia, his new life with her in a new country could have so easily backfired on him, he used to think he deserved nothing less but he had always had good intuitions about people and when he first spoke to Celia over the phone he felt a connection he hadn't felt since, well, since he'd first spoke to Jess. He tried not to pursue it but when things happen so seamlessly, the conversations flow and the person you speak to seems so intriguing and exciting, it's a difficult temptation to fight. Although he would never admit it to anybody outside of his and Celia's bed, he knew being with Celia was the best thing he had ever done. He loved Toby, God knows it tore him apart making that decision to leave him, and he knew he would always love Jess, but Celia ignited something in him that he never knew he had, when he was with her he was present, Jess had said that she often felt he was somewhere else, he used to make a joke of it and name places like Mars, Singapore or Morrisons car park as his current place, but with Celia he was there right alongside her, living every moment. Obviously, their relationship had a cloud of guilt over it, to some parts of the family she would always be the other woman, but it was working and anybody close to him saw that and couldn't begrudge him of happiness. Jess among them. She had her new man back in England, she didn't say much about him but Brian understood she was superstitious and wouldn't want to tempt fate by saying how good it was, maybe she would never admit it to Brian, it was clear they still cared for each other and the last thing either of them wanted was some 'my life's better than yours' competition.

It had all worked out for the best.

Jess was amazed how Toby was when he spoke to Brian, usually it followed a similar pattern, Toby would jump in with his headlines, his excitement would overflow and he would have to be reminded to calm down, to slow down, to tell his dad one thing at a time but he would go off at a tangent and his sentences would blur into lots of snippets of news at once. Then Jess would ask how things were in Vancouver, she would ask after Celia – something that had become easier over time and Jess was beginning to think Celia was really quite sweet, nobody had forced her to take time out to speak to Brian's ex-wife and son, it would have been easier for her not to, but she cared enough about him to recognise that Brian came with baggage and, to be fair to Toby, he was really sweet too.

Finally, the serious things came into the conversation, news about the family Brian chose to leave, asking about each other's jobs and then, of course, the wedding.

It was strange speaking so openly about the wedding but it became obvious that once it was brought out into the open, it could be discussed in an adult way. There was no jealousy from Jess, she joked about hoping Celia knew what she was getting herself into, was looking forward to seeing Celia in a wedding dress (she even complimented her figure, which Celia thanked her for) and said that she was slowly picking up extra shifts at work to buy the plane tickets so warned the couple not do it too quickly otherwise she'd have to buy a boat and row there herself.

Toby told his dad he had a picture to show him that he drew at school so he left the room, while he was gone Brian asked Jess if she was ok, he didn't know if it was the lighting or the video connection, but he thought she had looked like she was losing weight. Jess blushed and told him all this wedding talk had put her body into some kind of shock and she was unconsciously going on a wedding diet to fit into the dress she was planning to wear. Both Brian and Celia laughed but Brian knew Jess too well to be palmed off so easily, Jess looked unwell and he made a mental note to call when Celia was out lunching with friends and Toby was in bed.

Toby returned with an A4 piece of paper with a drawing of a cart on it. He explained Jim had a cart with wheels you can't pop and he had an umbrella that he used as a roof. He said Jim often let him fill it with tools and drag it around the garden to keep Jim from going backwards and forwards to the shed, apparently his knees weren't as good as they used to be so any help was appreciated. Toby said his knees thanked him for it.

"And how is Dean?" Brian piped up.

"Dean's Dean – Toby answered – he's listening at the door"

Jess spun her head at Toby and looked at him in disbelief.

"Toby?" Jess said.

"I hope I'll get to speak to him before the wedding, it's difficult enough trying to meet everybody, let alone new people on the day." Brian said keeping it light.

Celia gripped Brian's hand and an atmosphere came over the conversation, a coldness so stark it covered the time difference and geographical span in seconds.

Jess heard someone move from the doorway and she knew Dean was moving away. She shuddered at the thought of what this will lead to tonight, she was too tired for another argument and she was aware she hadn't won one in months and the cost of losing was quickly becoming too much to bear.

Jess sat with Toby as she was settling him down for bed, he knew something was wrong but he had no idea it was something he had done, Jess naturally tried to protect him so she wasn't about to blame him for some silly comment earlier. It was Dean's fault. Toby, without knowing had given Dean a way into the conversation, he could have come in, made a joke about listening at keyholes and said hello to Celia and Brian. His reluctance to speak to Brian had become an elephant in the room, why hadn't Jess introduced her boyfriend to them? Was she ashamed of him? Brian had joked that maybe he had two heads and no nose, but the truth was she *was* ashamed of Dean and, in a way, he did have two heads, well, two faces anyway, but she knew for Brian and Celia he would have been the happy, friendly version of Dean, the Dean who was everyone's friend, loved by all and a cheeky chappie who worked hard and drank harder, but was 'alright'.

Only a select few knew the other side.

Plus, Jess has a desire for Dean to be out of her life by the time the wedding came around, she's not broken yet, not entirely anyway, there is still fight inside her and that fight is fuelled by her son.

"Who are these people mum?" Toby asked showing her the photo of the children.

Jess looked at the photo and found herself transported back in time, she hadn't looked at this picture in so long, it was like meeting an old acquaintance in the street, she had come face to face with someone she hadn't seen in years but had a history with.

"Good lord" she said gently taking the photo and sitting beside Toby on the bed.

She spent a few moments looking and a smile formed on her face, Toby instinctively smiled too.

"These children, – she started – well, these children were living with a couple in Weston-Super-Mare. They were all in foster care. I haven't seen this in ages, I wonder where they are now. Look at these faces." She journeyed down memory lane, she remembered the sounds of the house, the smell of washing, the general activity of people living together, there were children running here and there, one was sitting on the sofa, another in the kitchen making a drink, it seemed children could appear from every nook and corner.

"What is Weston-Super…?"

"It's a town near the seaside, well it's actually *on* the seaside, there is a pier and donkeys that children can ride on, I took you there a long time ago, we had ice cream on the beach and you dropped half of it in the sand. You cried like mad so your dad swapped his for yours so you would stop. This is where you used to live, that baby is you." She handed the photo back and Toby looked at it with new eyes.

"That's me?" he said amazed.

"Yes, you lived there for a few months until we were told we could meet with you, the girl holding you was called Millie, she loved you to bits and was so upset when you left. She was a lovely girl. Had a voice like a jazz singer."

"Jazz singer?"

"It's a long story, but her voice was croaky" Jess smiled.

Jess looked at the photo and she found herself wondering about her life from that moment on, meeting that chubby little bundle of joy changed her life forever, it would be easy to sit and question every choice, leaving the North of England to relocate to the South where the jobs were easier to find and where most of Brian's clients were based. Oh well, no point bemoaning the wrong choices, now she had to concentrate on the positives, she still had Toby, Brian was still on the end of a, admittedly very long, phone line and she was still working and juggling school runs and keeping a home in order. There was just one thunderstorm in her skies and he had yet to say or do anything about Toby's comment to Brian earlier, that was still to come, Dean hated being embarrassed and called-out on things and Toby saying he was listening at the door would have consequences. Toby knew something was wrong too, he had noticed his mum was jittery and wondered if it was something he had done, he didn't think it was, but he also knew that Dean could fly off the handle at a second's notice. He knew the best way to help his mum (other than building a spaceship and taking her away) was to be good and go to bed without any drama or fuss.

He fell to sleep quickly, which was surprising given the noise that was coming from downstairs, Dean was angry but measured, which had become more frightening than when he would simply explode. The explosions came and went in a flash. They were out of his control and reactionary but, when he spoke like this, he simmered and bubbled and allowed the anger to increase in heat until it had so much momentum that nothing could contain it. He made Jess feel weak and beaten and told her in such a way that she understood completely that he knew she still loved Brian. He told her that she would never love someone like she loved her ex-husband and that he had tried time and time again to find a slither of room in her heart but she would never allow it. She fought him constantly and all of his best efforts were wasted because of how she still wanted her ex.

At first Jess quietly denied these accusations, she had to pick her response and the timings of these carefully, each one was met with further anger. How could Dean ever become part of Jess and Toby's life if neither of them truly accepted him? It was unfair what she was doing to him, Dean wanted to be Jess's soulmate, Brian made a fool of her by moving in with someone else behind her back, how he chose this other woman over his wife and son, was anybody's guess, she should have been livid.

"He made you a laughing stock" Dean said in mock sympathy.

Jess looked at him with confusion, was this all about jealousy? Was Dean simply just trying to replace Brian? Jess had no time to think any further before Dean went on.

"He left you and Toby to fend for yourself, you would never get by on your wage alone, if it hadn't been for me coming along, you'd be on the streets or back up North. You should be thankful to me." He added shaking his head.

Dean was actually feeling sorry for Jess, this was her fault, it was *her* making Dean so angry that he lashed out, she drove him to this, if she would just love him like she loved that bastard in Canada, this would be a happier place, and Toby, well Toby was a speed bump, a distraction, the sooner he was gone the better. Dean looked at Toby and saw hatred, he didn't like Toby at all. If he was able to get away with it, Toby would get more than a few bruises and the odd graze to his knees. Toby would disappear. No one would care, Dean justified, he was just another statistic of the country's foster children. He would be replaced in a day or two and easily removed from the database with the click of the delete button. That's how it worked, he had no blood relatives, no one would look for him if he didn't come to school one day, but people would soon be knocking on the door accusing Dean of doing him in. The busy bodies like those two next door would be right at the front waving a noose and looking for the nearest tree to swing Dean from, but they don't live here, they don't see the little shit sitting in front of the television watching that stupid programme, practicing tying knots with a short piece of string from the garden, rubbing pieces of wood together. Who cares the kid can start a fire, he's horrible, anybody that spends more than a few hours with him can see that.

Dean's mind was going into overdrive, his thoughts quickly turned to fantasy, of hurting Toby, *really* hurting Toby, doing something permanent. Jess stood up and walked to the window to close the curtains, Dean grabbed her arm, spun her and punched her in the stomach, Jess fell to the ground coughing and gasping for air. Dean looked down at her with no feeling. Look what she made him do again. Why can't she *stop* antagonising him? *She* knows he has a temper but she keeps pushing those buttons, goading him, tempting him to strike out.

He kicks her in the ribs and walks upstairs to Toby's room.

Toby was dreaming about a boat on the river, a brown duck cruises gently on the cool, flat surface. No ripples or reflection, the river is a large silver expanse. Toby's boat makes almost no sound aside from the quiet lapping of water on wood, he could feel the slight breeze but heard no other birds apart from the duck. Soon, some young chicks join their mother and she begins teaching them how to reach down beneath the surface for food, her short yellow legs peeking out, making Toby smile.

A swan was nearby, its large white body dwarfing the much smaller duck, its long neck swooping onto the water to gather water and tipping its head back to drink. Suddenly the mother duck was yanked beneath the water by an unseen force under the surface, it had a brief second to make a noise and try to extend its wings but it was too sudden, the duck was swallowed up with only a ripple remaining. Its chicks swam around in circles, each going in a different direction, looking for its mother. Toby realises the chicks would have difficulty surviving without its mother and he begins to grow concerned, the swan double backed towards them and seems to smile at the chicks as they chirp and flap.

Toby was woken by someone gripping his wrist and pulling him from his bed, the momentum made his body spin forwards and he bumped his head into something firm, it was Deans stomach. Dean picked him up and threw him onto the floor, Toby's arm crunched beneath his body and he felt pain run from his shoulder to his fingertips. He immediately spun onto his back and kicked his legs, scuttling backwards away from Dean who was standing above him in the dark, his huge form silhouetted from the light on the landing. Toby could hear his own feet scuffing the carpet, pushing further and further from Dean but his back was against the wall, he took a split second to realise his hands were gripping the carpet and he wondered why the carpet was so cold, cold travels downwards he thought to himself, heat travels upwards. His mind drifted to a basic science lesson he had at school when the teacher lit a candle and

held a feather above the flow of heat, the feather moved, Toby remembered saying wow.
Along with the thought was the sound of moving feet, god they were moving fast, his mind recognised the sound before he understood it completely, someone was racing up the stairs, they were moving faster than he ever could and by the time he'd thought this his mum was sprinting across the landing, her face red and angry, he had heard the expression 'if looks could kill...' before and now he understood it, if looks could indeed kill, Dean would be laying on the floor next to him dead.
Jess ran into the back of Dean with all the might and fury she could muster, she led with her shoulder and Toby saw her feet leave the ground, he had to move because Dean might fall on top of him.
But he didn't.
Dean moved forwards half a step and absorbed the blow.
If only his mum was heavier.
Dean grabbed Jess and punched her in the chest. The dull oomph as her breath exited her lungs was enough to send Jess back three or four steps, Dean followed her and grasped at her hair, Jess screamed and Dean tossed her into Toby's room and slammed the door shut.
Toby and Jess lay on the floor, each comforting the other. Their home was a prison but at least they had each other for company. Jess fell into a restless sleep with her legs firmly pressed against the door, if Dean was to come back, he would have to move her first, and Toby laid awake, plotting. Seven-year-old boys rarely feel fury as deep as Toby but he had seen and experienced enough. He wondered what Brian would do if he knew what was going on, he wondered what the man on the television would do, he wondered what Craig and Emma and Lizzie would do and then among the dozen thoughts littering his mind, he made a decision.
His mum had always told him if he couldn't do something then he should go back and start again, this was what he was going to do.

Dean wasn't in the house when Jess and Toby woke. Jess made Toby some breakfast and they ate in silence each alone with their thoughts. Jess didn't know how much Toby understood about what was going on but she knew he couldn't live in this environment anymore, neither of them could. Things had to change but she also knew she couldn't change things on her own, she needed help but her stupid pride was getting in the way, she needed to ask for help or things would never get better. She wondered where she would find it, she had friends but no one close enough for her to bother with this. The internet would have details on where to look and who to contact, charities for support, places for her and Toby to stay, but Dean checked all internet use and she couldn't very well leave the house. She found it hard to breath, she was sure she didn't have any broken bones but she was sore and wasn't strong enough mentally or physically to go very far. She didn't feel like she could call her family, they had their own lives and most of them were elderly. The same could be said for Jim and Cath, she couldn't burden them with this, she knew Cath didn't like Dean and she didn't feel like having a 'I told you so' conversation, Jim was no match for Dean and it would escalate into a fight within seconds, she wasn't about to let more people get hurt by Dean.

But she had to get Toby away, whatever happened to her was nothing compared to what was happening to her son.

"Thanks for helping me mum" Toby said as he munched on a piece of toast.

Jess looked at Toby and started to cry, a deep sobbing on hearing the words from Toby who she, his mother, had put in danger.

"It's ok Toby. I love you. You know that don't you?" She said rubbing his head.

"Yeah. I know. I love you too." He answered.

"I'm going to have a shower, come and wait in your room if you like" Toby nodded and followed his mum up the stairs, he looked at the cupboard and wondered when he would be spending another night in there, Dean was gone for now but if history taught them anything, it's that he wasn't done, he'd be back begging forgiveness and convincing Jess that he had changed.

Toby heard the shower running and did something he'd never done before, he walked into his mum and Dean's room and picked up his mum's phone. Occasionally she let him play games on there, it was a great help if she wanted him to sit still in a waiting room or at an appointment. He knew the pin number and he quickly accessed her text messages. He scrolled down and found 'Brian', it was a text message from a few weeks before, it said "ok, great, I'll let Toby know. Jess". Toby wrote; "Dad its toby things are bad I won't to talk" He pressed send and put the phone back where he found it.

He went into the garden and sat at the top near the hedge, Jim wasn't out there but he could see Cath in the kitchen window, she was busy washing things up, she looked up, noticed him and then rushed out into the garden.
"Toby, are you ok?" She was almost running towards him.
Toby stood up and said hello, he asked where Jim was.
Just as he said this Jim appeared and walked up to where they were, he was looking very worried, Toby wondered if something bad had happened, and then he remembered, it dawned on him that Jim and Cath had heard everything.
"Oh thank God Toby, are you ok? Where's Jess?" Toby explained that she was inside having a shower, he told them that Dean wasn't there and they had a big fight last night.
"We know, we heard" Jim said gravely.
"We should have called the police, I said there was something very wrong, that Dean is a monster, he should be locked up!" Cath said angrily.
Jim knelt down and put his hand on Toby's shoulder and asked if he was ok or if he was hurt.
Toby asked if he could stay in the garden for a while and just play a little with Jim's cart, of course Jim agreed. Cath crossed the low fence and went into Jess's back door, Toby and Jim both heard her call Jess's name as she went in.
Jim turned to Toby and said "it's ok Tobes, Cath will help your mum, she might look old but she's got the heart of a buffalo".

Once Jim had explained what a buffalo was, Toby felt a little better and wished his mum was a buffalo the night before when she ran into Dean.

"Jim, can I ask a question?" Toby asked.

"Of course, anything"

"Where is Weston-Super-Mare?"

Chapter Thirteen – Preparation

Toby had so much to think about, Jim had told him that Weston Super Mare was a little over twenty miles away to the west (and down a bit) but how could he get there without causing suspicion, and how could he get his mum to come with him? He wasn't about to leave his mum to cope with Dean on her own, she would surely get his share of punishments and when he thought of Dean throwing his mum in the cupboard it made him angry.

At its most basic, every journey required at least two things; a destination and the means to get there.

He knew a little about reading a map, and his compass was primed and ready to go, but if he planned it sensibly he would need to leave at night so nobody saw him, which would mean navigating by the stars, but he hadn't done that, every time he planned to wake up in the night and look out of his bedroom two things inevitably happened. The first was the stars were too difficult to see, his street had enough light pollution to prevent any budding astronomer from carrying on with their hobby, and, secondly, he'd sleep straight through. He knew Jim's cart would be perfect for his expedition, it was large enough to carry anything he would need and also large enough for him to rest in if he got tired. He didn't know how far twenty miles was but the way Jim said it, it was too far to walk in a day. This would need more planning than he knew how to do.

Toby was still in the garden chatting to Jim, who had gone into the house to find some maps of the area between Bristol and Weston-Super-Mare, Toby asked if Jim could maybe print some off for him so he could put them on his bedroom wall. He told Jim about how he used to live in Weston with another family and his first friend lived there, a girl called Millie. She had blonde hair and was in a photograph that Toby liked looking at. He was going to tell Jim that he wanted to go there and take his mum with him so they could stay there but he decided against it, Jim was old and there was no way he would understand.

Jim had grown to regard Toby as a kind of grandson, he did the things that young grandsons did, he helped in the garden, he was limitless in his enthusiasm for helping and learning about the different tools and they would give each other presents. Jim cared for Toby much more than he thought he ever could and over these short years he had learnt things about himself that he never thought he would. He possessed emotions that he didn't know he had and he wasn't about to dash Toby's dreams of escape. So what, Toby thought he could simply run away with his mum to somewhere safe? God only knows the things that young boy had seen in his short life, he had a bad start as it was, his mum was no role model and he had lost her so early. Jess and Brian were his second go at a happy life and then that dissolved when Brian left, Jim knew that had hit Toby hard, he loved his dad and Brian was strict but also tender for his son, it broke Jim and Cath's heart when they heard the family was breaking up and then this idiot had come along to make things worse. Jim had never formally met Dean, Cath said hello to him once and immediately judged him (correctly as it turned out) as a bad one. But it was none of their business, what went on in someone's own home was up to them, Jim and Cath had made a life of not sticking their noses into other people's problems but this was different, this was bad for everyone and from the things they sometimes heard, things had gotten worse overnight.

If Toby wanted to go to Weston-Super-Mare, he'd gladly fill the car with sandwiches and a bucket and spade and take Toby there, Jess could come too if she wanted too, if it meant keeping them away from that psychopath for a day, he'd do it. But he had the feeling that Toby was planning some great journey, maybe it was a kneejerk reaction to the things that had gone on in that house. Jim wanted to tell Toby that it was a hair-brained plan but Toby was young and there was no way he would understand.

Jess poked her head out of the kitchen and called for Toby. As Toby reached the backdoor Jess asked him what he had done on her phone, his dad had been phoning her and had left a message saying he hoped everything was ok because Toby had text him.

He had been phoning every few minutes.
Toby said he wanted to talk his to dad, Jess bit her lip and looked at Cath for advice, "I think it's a good idea, he's been through a lot, he probably wants a friend to speak to" she said.
Jess reluctantly passed him her phone.
Toby went into his room and dialled his dad's number, a few seconds later he was speaking to Vancouver, the line was ok but had a strange echo like he was talking in the bathroom.

"Did I do the right thing?" Jess said to Cath looking up at the ceiling as if she could look through the floor and into Toby's room.
"I've no idea but he obviously wanted to speak to him. Has he ever taken your phone before?"
"Not that I know of, he's not really a technical child, he's more bows and arrows in the woods."
Cath laughed and agreed, if there was one thing Toby loved, it was being outside getting dirty and identifying trees and plants.

Upstairs Toby was speaking to his dad and opening up like a book, everything was laid bare, every painful detail revealed, Brian couldn't believe what he was hearing but somehow things fell into place and suddenly little quirks and niggles made sense. Dean never wanted to speak to Brian, Jess was losing weight, it wasn't illness, it was that bastard. Brian did his best to remain calm, two people that he cared about, had shared a life with were being abused. He didn't dare think about the damage this was doing to Toby. And Jess? From what Toby said it sounded like Jess had been raped as well as beaten.
He had called for Celia and had put Toby on speaker phone, he hadn't asked Toby to repeat what he had already said, Toby was audibly holding back tears and having to repeat it would be cruel, and Toby had suffered enough. Celia stood with her hand over her mouth in shock. I know I've said this before but Celia was a good woman, she understood the problem in a moment and in the next had worked out the logical next step, she was online in a few moments and looking at flights to the UK.

Brian looked at Celia and half smiled, it seemed he was going back to England sooner than expected.

Jim was sitting with his wife and Jess in the kitchen while Toby spoke to his dad, he was holding a printed map in his hand but neither Jess or Cath payed any attention to them, they were both listening for Toby. Eventually he came down and returned the phone to his mum.
"Dad says he's going to come home as soon as he can."
Jess sat shocked, a dozen thoughts in her mind, Cath and Jim felt relief that the fight wasn't hers to fight alone. They could now phone for help, Jess didn't want the police involved, but she was happy to speak to someone about what had happened. There was so much happening in such a short space of time that she barely had a moment to think properly.
Toby had left the kitchen and was walking up his garden path, he stepped over the low fence and made his way towards Jim's shed, he knew exactly what he was looking for, he'd seen it a few weeks ago tucked away behind the lawnmower next to the cart.
Polystyrene.
The man on the television said that this white material - that seemed to be made of a billion tiny white bubbles - was great for sleeping on, he had a show where he was on a coastline and some washed up on the beach, he slept on it under a roof made of leaves and said he was lucky to have found such a treasure because it makes a terrific insulator. Toby had seen that episode three or four times and recognised it when he had seen it in Jim's shed a few months ago. It had come with a washing machine that they had replaced and Jim had kept it. Now it was Toby's turn to be lucky to have found such a treasure.

Over the next few hours, things moved very fast, so much needed to be done but without realising it Toby had been planning for this development for ages. You could argue that the first step was getting the torch and, once that was acquired, Toby had been quietly and methodically putting a kit together for an expedition. He had the means to get there and now he had the destination.

He went to his bedroom and put some things into his school bag, he took some clothes, his water bottle, the compass his dad had given him, some sticks that he had under his bed that were particularly good for creating the beginnings of a fire, the photo of his baby self, the bundle of letters from his father and Harold. Harold would be crucial on this journey, he might have been quiet and awful in a crisis, but he was still Toby's right-hand man and he was sure if, when needed, Harold would reveal his true talent and possibly even save the day.

Toby took a piece of paper and a felt tip pen and started to write his mum a letter, he knew she would be worried and it was only polite to let her know where he was going. He wasn't deserting her, not by any means, she had to come too, but who would be there when his dad came home? His dad would worry if, upon returning home, the house was empty, he might even get back into the taxi and go back to the airport to catch the next plane to Canada. A wasted journey. Toby wrote he was going to Weston Super Mare, he would be fine, Harold was with him and he had Jim's cart to keep things in, he would camp out and if it rained, he would put up the umbrella. He told her he took some clothes from his drawers and he had a small stash of money (he didn't tell her how and where he got it, she wouldn't be very happy about that) and he added that he had taken some food too. He hadn't done this yet, but he was going to. He folded the letter and put it in his pocket.

Jim, Cath and Jess were still downstairs and he could hear his mum talking on the phone to somebody, he couldn't quite hear what they were saying but Jess was nodding with her hand on her forehead and the other voice was a female. Toby saw a folded piece of paper on the table, it must have been the map Jim had printed for him, perfect, another piece was falling into place. Toby took the map and, thinking it was a good a place as any to put his letter for his mum, folded it in half and put it in the same spot.

He stuffed the map into his bag and headed to Jim's shed.

He took out the map and quickly looked at it, it all seemed pretty straight forward, twenty-two miles to Weston Super Mare, he would pull the cart up the hills and then jump in it and ride down the other side, it wouldn't take long. He would have to sleep in the cart, but, it would be fine, it would be like going to the big shop but forty times, that seemed simple enough. Putting the map into one of the pockets at the front of the cart Toby looked up at a shelf and saw a knife, he knew he needed a knife, he might have to set traps to catch food (he hoped not, he didn't like the thought of eating an owl or rabbit) and a knife seemed to be so useful, he could cut small branches or string, yes, he would need a knife. He selected two, one was a silver one with a triangular blade, it was short but he knew it was very sharp, both Jim and Brian owned one and both told him it was so sharp it would cut his finger off. He put that in his bag with a great deal of care. The second was one Jim used to cut down branches in the garden, it was slightly curved with big jagged teeth like a saw, it folded into itself but it would do the jobs the sharp one couldn't do. He'd need his fingers so he needed a second knife.

Toby had a few more things to do before he set off, getting more supplies was top of the list.

He headed off to the big shop again, he'd love to be able to buy a fishing rod and line but he wasn't sure if he would need it until he got to the seaside and then he would prefer the fish in the golden batter anyway so it was a waste of time. He thought he would buy some water, some bananas, other items of food and some sweets. He also bought a ball of gardening string; he had no idea if he would need it but the television man was always using tying things up so why not.

As he exited the shop, he could see Emma, the police officer, chatting to a group of teenagers, this probably meant Craig was nearby, and where you found Craig, you always find Lizzie.

Jess put the phone down and immediately Cath put her hand on her shoulder, "that was incredibly brave Jess" she said.
"I feel such a fool" Jess said.

"Nonsense, there's no fools in this house, the only fool that was here is gone. Hopefully for good, why if I was twenty years younger…" Jim started.
"But you're not! - interrupted Cath – the last thing we need is more violence"
"That's all these people seem to understand" Jim was angry how he had lived next door to this going on for so long and only now something was getting done, and it wasn't how he would choose to settle it. But he understood he wasn't a match for a man thirty years his junior, but it still didn't stop him thinking about how much he'd enjoy seeing Dean getting a good hiding.
Jess stood and instinctively looked into the garden for her son, "He was here a while ago" Cath said.
"I doubt he's causing much harm" Jim added.
Jess nodded and smiled slightly, Toby was the one constant in all of this, he was so brave but she wondered what lasting damage this would do. She reminded herself that she was doing something about it and not to dwell on the things that can't be changed, she should focus on what can be changed and she was making changes right now.
"I'll nip next door and see if I bump into him on the way - Jim said, he eyed the folded paper on the table – I'll take his map with me."
Jim left and returned to his house, Toby wasn't in either garden and he wasn't in the shed – Jim popped his head in to check – so he went into the house for a sit down. He wouldn't admit it to anybody, particularly Jess and Cath but he was tired, this recent upset had reminded him how old he was and how useless he was becoming. Time for a sit down with a cup of tea. He put the piece of paper on a pile of newspapers he kept by the back door, if Toby didn't want it, and it appeared he didn't, he'd recycle it or use it to start a bonfire in the autumn.

Toby was busy making a fuss of Lizzie, Craig was hoping he'd bump into this little lad again, he'd started to enjoy seeing a friendly face. Emma was continuing to read the riot act to the teenagers who nodded and looked at the ground, Craig could tell by their body language that they were no bother, they weren't career criminals in the making and a telling off from a police officer was all they needed. One day they'd probably look back on this day and laugh, on the whole most teenagers were ok, it didn't hurt to have a chat with them from time to time and, as long as the group wasn't large (teenagers seemed to find extra courage from being in large groups) Emma could handle it on her own.

Craig looked down at Toby and asked something that had been bothering him since meeting the boy, "You're here on your own aren't you Toby?" he tried to ask it in his most gentle voice, spooking the boy might make him run and that wasn't what Craig wanted.

Toby looked down and nodded.

"Do you always come here on your own?"

He nodded again.

"Toby, do you have someone at home looking after you?" Craig hated this question and, truth be told, he was dreading the answer.

"My mum is at home" Toby looked into Craig's eyes, Craig knew this was the truth and let out a little breath of relief.

"Is your mum unwell? Are you looking after her by getting her shopping?" There were hundreds of young people in the country looking after unwell adults, they would do everything they could on top of going to school, their social life was non-existent and it was no way for a child to live, Craig knew of such cases and had even helped these people get assistance, Toby seemed to fit the criteria.

Toby shook his head.

Craig decided to give Lizzie a treat, sometimes silence was a powerful prompt, if Toby wanted to speak, he could, maybe he would stay silent too and Craig would never set eyes on this sad, but determined, boy again. Maybe Toby would start talking about Lizzie or something totally removed like the weather or the average weight of a new-born sealion, but the choice was his.

"My mum is sad, she has a boyfriend that hurts her, I hear her crying sometimes at night, I know he's hurting her and it makes me cry that

I can't help." Toby cried, little tears running down his cheeks and gathering on his chin.

Emma was approaching out of the corner of Craigs vision, he looked to her and gave her a look that she immediately recognised as she shouldn't come closer, not yet, he was talking to Toby and he was telling him something. Something important.

She stopped in her tracks and changed direction, she walked to a bench and sat down.

"Does he hurt you?"

Toby nodded and looked down further, his shoulders jerking as he cried silent sobs. Craig had heard dozens of stories like this, it never gets easier and his reaction is always the same, anger, but controlled, police-trained anger.

"What kind of thing does he do Toby?"

Toby said nothing.

"You don't have to say anything to me Toby, I won't be upset, you can stay here and give Lizzie a big cuddle if you prefer. She really likes you; she's got a good instinct for nice people." Craig stroked Lizzie, who, as you can imagine was enjoying the attention, sitting in the back of a police van was no match for actual physical contact with someone with seemingly endless strokes and fuss.

"He puts me under the stairs"

"That sounds awful, why does he do that?" Craig asked.

"I don't really know, once I wanted a drink and he caught me so I went in there. He pushes me over and he doesn't let me eat tomato ketchup, he punched mum and she slept in my room and kept the door closed so he wouldn't come back. He was going to hurt me but she rescued me and he hit her. He hit her so hard. I thought she was dead. I thought Dean had killed my mum"

Craig opened his arms and Toby rushed into them, Toby was tiny, there was almost no weight to him, like holding a baby bird, he was weightless and helpless.

Craig started mentally drawing up a list of people he could contact and put Toby's mum in touch with, there was help out there for her, she would be put somewhere else tonight with Toby so this Dean can't continue to do what he does, he was making the plan, resisting the temptation to go to Toby's house and arrest this bastard, he knew things had to follow a certain procedure, things go wrong if the correct protocol isn't adhered. This had to be done correctly.

Craig moved Toby and looked him in the eye, "Is Dean there at the moment?"

Toby shook his head, sniffed and told Craig what had happened during the last twenty-four hours. Dean nodded and looked at Emma and gave her the green light to come over. Craig filled her in and Toby received another hug.

Toby was certain his mum didn't want the police involved, she had said that to Jim and Cath, Toby felt like he had somehow betrayed his mum by telling the police, but Craig was friendly, Toby felt safe around him and knew his mum needed help in doing this. Home was horrible, it used to be his favourite place, where he was happiest but Dean had ruined all of that, he didn't feel safe there anymore and after last night, his mum wasn't safe there either.

"You can't tell my mum, she doesn't want the police around when Dean is there, it would make Dean more angry and he would be more unkind to mum" Toby said looking at the officers.

"But Toby, we can help, you've done the best thing. Telling us will go a long way to making things better at home, we can deal with Dean." Craig said gently.

"Craig's right – Emma joined in, putting her hand on Toby's shoulder – there is an army of people whose job it is to help people like you and your mum."

Toby wasn't sure, he had never seen an army before, an army was more people than he could ever count, how would they suddenly turn up to help his mum? That would also take time, and time was something that Toby felt they didn't have, Dean would be home any day and he still had to get to the seaside so he could find them a place to live.

"Don't do anything. Please." Toby said to Craig.

Craig frowned and looked at Emma, she could see the questions in his eyes and knew the best thing to do was to keep him calm, Craig was a good man, and he had a soft spot for damsels in distress, she immediately recognised in him someone who wanted to save everybody, but she knew that was impossible. Some people are too far gone to be saved while others just don't get the chance to save themselves, often all it takes is some kindness or someone taking a chance on them, she had no idea what kind of person Toby's mum was, by the sound of it she was just someone who simply invited the wrong person in. This happened a lot, she'd seen it dozens of times. They say that everyone is a few bad choices away from losing everything, and it's true, another thing that was true was that Craig had no intention in leaving things alone, this was a clear damsel in distress and Craig would put in the extra work needed to save her. Her choice now was simple; does she go along with it, or attempt to reign him back?

Toby made his way home and wondered how he would start his journey, the day was getting away from him, it was too late to start now, it would be dark before he had made it to the edge of town and he would be looking for a place to sleep.
He decided he would go first thing in the morning.
Toby remembered that Jim and Cath often visited a garden centre a few miles away, maybe he could hitch a ride with them, the cart would easily fit into Jim's boot and they could drop him off and, another great idea, he could nip into the garden centre, use their toilet, grab something to eat and then set off. His plan was coming together so nicely, he smiled for the first time that day at how easily things seemed to be working out for him. He would go home, pack the remaining things into Jim's shed and ask Jim about the lift.

He was putting his sleeping bag near his things in the shed when he saw Jim in the house, he was talking to Cath and they were involved in a very serious conversation, Cath was saying something and Jim was agreeing and saying things back, it was probably best not to disturb them, adults didn't like being disturbed, he could see him in the morning to arrange the lift.

That night he could hardly wait to go to bed, he had packed everything in Jim's shed and all he needed to do was get up, get dressed, grab some breakfast and go next door. He heard his mum go into her room and it sounded like she was getting ready for bed too, maybe she needed the rest. Before Cath had left, she told Toby that his mum needed a good night's sleep and plenty of rest, fair enough, he can do that, he had other things on his mind anyway. Besides, it was all explained in the letter Toby had written for her.

Craig was just finishing his shift; he'd finished writing the last of the paperwork and was making his way from the locker room to the exit when he heard Emma calling him.
"So, what's the plan?" she asked him.
"Plan? Plan for what? I'm off home to watch some television and get some shut eye" he replied.
"You know what I mean, about Toby?" She looked seriously at him.
Craig returned her gaze and simply shrugged "there's not a lot I can do, the boy has asked me to leave well alone, I can't really go against his wishes, can I?"
Emma raised her eyebrows, "that doesn't sound like you"
"Well what can I do? I'd love to go in there and sort things but it sounds like a mess, we don't even know anything about his home life, for all I know, his mum gives as good as she gets. I can't go around believing everything every child says"
"But you do, don't you?" Emma said.
"Yes, I do. I think you do too."
Emma nodded.
"It wouldn't hurt to maybe drive past there at some point, see what's going on. We patrol near there anyway." Emma added.
Craig smiled and new she'd help him, he was glad she would, he didn't trust himself in these positions, he always jumped in head first and seemed to make matters worse, she was the one with the soft hands, she diffused situations better than him, together they were like a hammer and a scalpel.

"Maybe we could take Lizzie there tomorrow, let her sniff around on the grass for a bit, no harm in that is there?" Craig suggested.
"Exactly right, but we don't know his address, so it might take a while"
"No problem there, I wrote his address down a few weeks ago, it's Brook Gardens, number nineteen." He smiled.
"You write everything down, don't you?" Emma smiled back.
"Old school Em, old school."
They went outside and went their separate ways.

Chapter Fourteen – The Tooth in The Front Lawn

Toby was awake and dressed in no time, it was a little later than he would have liked but when he looked out of the window, he could see Jim's car still on the driveway. He rushed downstairs and started eating his breakfast, he was a little slow at making it, he needed to stand on a chair to reach the cereal, and the milk in the fridge was heavier than expected, but he was able to make it ok. He tried to eat it slowly so he didn't get tummy ache – adults were always telling him to slow down when he ate, they threatened he would get a tummy ache, but he never did - his friend George once ate lots of ice cream before immediately heading to the trampoline, he was sick and the other children ran screaming towards the safety of their parents while George's embarrassed mother cleaned it up – in between mouthfuls he was putting on his boots, looking out of the window for Jim's car and trying to get going.

His mum came downstairs and immediately switched on the kettle.
"You're up early, going somewhere?" she asked.
"uh huh - he nodded, mouth full of breakfast, he finally swallowed – I'm going with Jim to the garden centre, I have to get to his house before he leaves"
"Oh, well, fair enough, Jim didn't say anything, but I guess aliens could land in the garden and I'd not notice at the moment. Do you want some money to spend?"
"No thanks, I've got some" Toby put his bowl in the sink, gave his mum a kiss and turned to go.
"Slow down – his mum called to his back – you'll get tummy ache"
Toby went through the garden, over the fence at the top, into Jim and Cath's, down towards the house and into the shed. His things were still there, nothing had been moved so it was time.
He took a deep breath, "this is it" he said to himself. He bent down and started unfolding the cart, he had to undo a large black plastic clip to release the legs but it popped up and he locked the parts in place with the little metal clips. This cart had to get him all the way to the seaside, he'd have to go across roads, paths, grass, mud and,

eventually, sand. He knew the cart could do it, but could he? Somewhere in all of the planning and preparation he had forgotten he was still a young boy, he had to stand on a chair to reach his breakfast for god's sake, could this be done? He wasn't someone who had a great deal of self-doubt, he'd seen his idol on television climb trees for food, shimmy down waterfalls to catch fish, build fires in the wind, fill holes with burning embers to cook food, this wasn't going to be as difficult as that. He'd be fine. He'd do one thing at a time and soon he'd reach the seaside, he grew strength from having a map and a compass, anything was possible if you had those things, after all a journey only needed was a destination and a means. He had both.
He was putting the final things in the cart and securing Harold to the back of the cart when he heard a car start.
Jim was leaving without him!
If he hadn't been busy doubting this whole venture, he would have been ready, if he had woken up when he had planned, he would be in the car that was pulling out of the driveway and trundling down the road.
Now what?
Jim wouldn't be home for another two hours at least.
There was nothing for it, he has to walk all the way.
With that thought, Toby set off.

Jess was in the lounge next door, if she had turned around at the right time, she would have seen her son walking down the road pulling a garden cart, she would have seen a large umbrella peeking out the rear, she would have seen her sons school bag and his purple and green sleeping bag and finally she would have seen his yellow rabbit staring back at her.
The truth was no one saw him, he walked out of Jim's driveway while Cath was indoors wondering about her neighbour's state of mind. Cath had wondered if Jim going out was the right thing, normally she would have joined him but she felt she would be happier at home, she would miss it just this once, be a shoulder for Jess if she needed

to talk or maybe take Toby off her hands if Jess needed to make some phone calls.

Toby carried on down the road, he passed his other neighbour who he had rarely seen, who worked such strange hours and would be away for days on end, coming back home in the early morning never to be heard or seen for weeks. He crossed roads, negotiated zebra crossings and made one final stop to the burger restaurant. It was too early to get food, he would have liked to have had a reserve supply of food to eat when he grew hungry but he knew there were lots of these restaurants along his route, he would be fine.

At the rear of the big shop were a number of bus stops, most went into town but some would take him closer to where he was heading, would it be foolish to risk being caught so soon after he had started? Toby thought so.

That was until he saw an elderly man standing at the bus stop with a young boy, why this could have been Toby and Jim. He started to read some of the bus notices, he knew different numbers went to different places, he wondered which one he needed to catch.

Well, if in doubt, ask. So, he did.

"Excuse me – he asked the elderly man – which bus goes to Whitchurch?"

The old man looked at Toby with kind eyes, "I think it's the number fifteen, it leaves from the stop over there, but ask the driver to make sure".

Toby thanked him and made his way across the road, his cart clattering behind him.

Pretty soon a bus appeared with the number fifteen above the driver's window.

Here we go, Toby thought.

At around this time Emma was finishing her cup of coffee and was immediately wondering where her next one would come from, she needed a caffeine fix before she started her shift, she knew today was going to be a strange day and was slightly anxious about it. Craig was already outside with Lizzie and he'd been chirpier than usual, it

normally takes him a few hours to warm up. Today he'd seemed like a boy expecting good news.
"We've got a call to go to the betting shop on Grosvenor Road, apparently they had some trouble there last night." Craig said.
"When did you want to head to Brook Gardens?" Emma asked.
"There's no rush, maybe we can fit it in before lunch?" Craig gestured for Lizzie to leap into the back of the car and he got in, a quick radio message to control and he started the engine.

Toby had paid for a ticket to Whitchurch, the driver had asked where his parents were, Toby - expecting this - told him that his granddad was picking him up from a stop along the way, this seemed to put the drivers mind at rest but he asked Toby to sit near the front of the bus. He said it was so Toby could keep an eye on his cart, but in truth he wanted to keep an eye on Toby. He made a note to radio back and tell him he had picked up an unaccompanied minor, you occasionally got people who seemed out of place or lost, this young boy didn't seem either of those things, he seemed assured and confident, but it didn't hurt to let people know.
All Toby had to do now was, as he drew closer to Whitchurch, look for a man at the bus stop and hope he doesn't get on as Toby gets off.

Jess was tidying the house and trying to keep herself busy, it paid to be busy at times like this, she was still sore from where Dean had punched her and every time it hurt she allowed it to, maybe she needed to be reminded what an awful person he was, but she would always conclude that she was worse for being so foolish. Maybe she deserved someone like this, no, that was stupid talk, she quickly reprimanded herself, what a thing to think, who on earth deserves someone like Dean? No one deserves that. It wasn't her fault, none of it was her fault. But the question still remained, when would Dean come back?
She was certain he would and she was more certain that he would not enter this house again, if he came back, she would stand in the

street if need be, letting him in would mean having to get him out again and she knew in her heart, she wasn't strong enough for that, although she hated him, she was still afraid of him and fear has a way of making people act differently. What was it that Mike Tyson used to say; everyone has a plan until they get hit. It's true, all of her thoughts and plans would soon go out the window once she saw him.

She decided to slide the bolt on the front door, Dean has a key but that wouldn't help if she slid the bolt, let him knock, let him feel like the outsider, this was her house after all, hers and Toby's. He was the interloper, the stowaway, the unwanted guest.

Cath popped her head around the back door and called if Jess was home – Jess made a note to lock the back door too.

"Morning Jess, how are you feeling today?" she asked.

Jess smiled and said she was ok considering, she asked if Toby and Jim got off ok and to please say they remembered the booster seat for the car.

Cath looked a little puzzled and said "He didn't mention Toby was going with him, sneaky devil, the onetime I don't go he finds a replacement. Typical. Out with the old eh?"

Jess smiled and offered a cup of tea. Cath accepted and it had the makings of a nice, calm Sunday.

Toby could feel the driver's eyes checking on him from time to time, he'd been on the bus for around fifteen minutes, people had gotten on and people had gotten off but still Toby sat in the second row back near the window. His cart had its brake on so was in no danger of sliding around but Toby couldn't help worry about Harold, he was sat there so exposed, anyone could take him, but he had to be calm, nothing could make the driver suspicious, this plan was saving time and distance. Toby couldn't walk as fast as a bus; it was just a pity he couldn't take the bus all the way to Weston-Super-Mare but he didn't have enough money and someone at some point would ask questions.

He was now in Whitchurch so Toby made a deliberate show of looking out of the window more keenly, the driver assumed he was looking for his granddad but, in truth, Toby was simply looking for anybody that fit the description.

The first stop was a young mother with a toddler and another child in a stroller, no that wasn't right, plus they got on the bus. The second stop was an elderly Indian couple, the man wore shiny shoes and the lady smelt of a perfume Toby hadn't smelt before, it was nice and reminded him of flowers that grew in Jim and Cath's garden. Another stop came and went and still no man to help complete the illusion. The bus drove along still and the driver started looking more frequently at Toby, he felt other eyes on him from the passengers, he had to get off the bus soon. The bus passed a man walking on the path and Toby looked at him and stood up, "that's him!" Toby announced, he reached for the bell and rang it. A hundred yards ahead, the bus slowed and stopped at the bus stop, Toby pulled his cart, fumbled for the brake and made his way off. He stopped and thanked the driver. The driver told him to have a good day and to keep out of mischief, Toby smiled and left, the cart rocked as it hit the pavement.

Toby stood by the bus stop, looking towards the old man who was drawing nearer and nearer, but the bus didn't pull away, was the driver waiting?

Toby waved to the old man and started walking towards him. The driver, satisfied that all was well, closed the doors and pulled away into the Sunday traffic.

It had worked, Toby had eaten into the miles and he was on the outskirts of town.

If Toby had turned to his left he would have seen a police car driving past him, two officers and a dog were in that car, one was planning on getting a coffee from one of the posher outlets and the other was wondering when a good time would be to visit nineteen Brook Gardens.

All was quiet at Brook Gardens, there were a few cars passing and the occasional pedestrian made their way along the pathways, but it was nearing lunch time and most would be home preparing food or snapping up last minute items from shops. Somewhere somebody was nursing the mother of all headaches and vowing never to drink again, some might be regretting the actions of the night before and waking up in a strange bed with a stranger beside them and wishing they hadn't given in to the nocturnal temptations of the heavy drinkers but life was for living and lessons would no doubt be learnt. It's one thing to order a twelve-inch margherita with extra pepperoni and jalapeños but quite another to start the day in someone else's bed. Sunday was a time for washing the car, visiting family, putting flowers on graves and perhaps preparing for the upcoming working week. It was a day for going to church, calling old friends, watching football in the pub, reading a newspaper with a pot of fresh coffee and weeding the garden. Sunday was the calm before the storm, the last bastion of joy before Monday jolted us awake and reminded us that money needed to be made to pay for the bills and the holidays and the lifestyle we strive for. Sunday was also the day that Dean decided to return to the street.

If this was an old cowboy movie, Dean would stride down the main street slowly and dangerous, people would close the shutters and bring children into the safety of the home, away from the upcoming fight. Undertakers would busy themselves measuring up the soon-to-be-corpses for coffins to be buried in the old graveyard at the foot of the hill. There would be a lone cry from a circling eagle that could almost smell the blood about to be spilt upon the dusty desert ground. But this wasn't a movie, this was real drama in a real street and it wouldn't stop when the director called "cut!"

Most of the inhabitants didn't know who this man was walking down their street, some would have seen him pass by in his white van on occasion, some might even say they recognised him, some might even claim he was living at number nineteen with that woman whose husband left her for a woman in Calcutta (gossip often resembles Chinese whispers and can gather momentum and wilder

details as it circulates). Dean looked like any normal man out for a stroll on a Sunday lunchtime, nothing to see here, move on, go about your business, but Dean was a man looking for a pardon, he liked living with Jess, she had most of what he wanted, hers was a place to rest, sleep, feed and live, if it wasn't for her boy and her annoying ways, he might go as far to say it was perfect being there. If it weren't for her pushing his buttons, his life would be pretty settled. It was time to go home. He'll apologise, he'll say he had no idea what came over him, he was out of line, he'd been under stress at work and it bubbled and boiled over in the wrong way. What could he do to make things better? To get things back to the way they were? How could he make her see that he didn't want any of this? This wasn't him, he was a laugh, he was a top bloke, sure he liked a drink and yes, he'll admit, he had a temper, but he had been pushed and pushed. He would say that he understood that she had a life before he had come along, that it was natural for her to have feelings for her ex, he understood that, you can't switch off a light and make everything disappear, in fact it was a credit to her as a woman that she was emotionally mature enough to accept her feelings for Brian but still be able to have a strong relationship with another man. He was confident and was looking forward to great make-up sex when he entered the front garden to number nineteen and slid his key into the lock to unlock the front door.
It opened half a centimetre and didn't budge any further.

"So, I take it the wedding will be in Vancouver" said Cath.
Her mug was on the table and, when drinking warm drinks together, her and Jess had sat chatting and gossiping for over an hour. Some relationships are based around and built upon the foundation of sharing a warm drink and putting the world to rights, women are particularly good at this kind of thing, truths are laid bare and emotions discussed over a simple cup of heated water and a spoon of coffee or bag of tea.

"I think so, I haven't wanted to ask too much, I'm the ex-wife, and that's how I'll be seen by everyone on the day." Jess cupped her cold mug in both hands and leant heavily on the table surface.
"And how do *you* feel?" Cath asked.
"Fine. I know that probably sounds hard, it's not like I don't like Brian, I do, of course I do, a part of me will always love him, but things have moved on and it's not as if I don't have enough around here to keep me occupied. Toby is a never-ending bundle of change, I wish Brian could have seen more of his growing up but he made a choice and, if I'm honest, I'm glad he stuck to it and it worked out."
"So, what is Celia like? Toby seems to like her"
"She's nice. Part of me wishes she wasn't but it makes things so much easier that she is. She totally accepts Toby; she has never got in the way of us speaking to Brian. Obviously, I wish she hadn't chosen my husband for a lover, but it's too late for that now. I'm actually looking forward to the wedding, I haven't been to Canada before, Toby will love it and it'll be nice to see Brian."
"It's definitely something to look forward to, I haven't been on a plane in years, I think the last time Jim took me away was – "
The front door was moved, Jess jumped out of her skin, Cath felt herself go cold, it was Dean. All Cath could think was it was typical that her husband wasn't here, he had no mobile phone so couldn't be contacted, blast his technophobe ways.
Jess moved quickly to the front door and was surprised by her strength when she shouted "go away Dean, you're not welcome". She couldn't believe she had said it, her voice was shaking and didn't disguise her fear, but she had said it alright.

Toby was sitting on a low wooden fence by a park, he had parked the cart near him and he was sat with his feet crossed eating a banana, he had been walking for a little while and, if his map reading was worth anything, he had covered quite a big chunk of the route. He tried to work out how much there was still to go but every time he tried, he got a little depressed so decided to simply enjoy his banana and put the map safely back in the pocket of the cart. The sky was a little grey, no sign of rain or rain clouds but there was no blue either, he would have preferred a blue sky to keep him warm and his spirits up, but he was pleased with what he had accomplished so far. He kept reminding himself that this was the furthest from home he'd ever been on his own. It was only a few weeks ago that he went to the big shop, now here he was enjoying food he bought himself whilst sitting in a park that he'd never seen before. The man from the television would be proud. Harold was proud, he could see him poking out from his seat. He put the banana skin in the cart (he wasn't going to throw it on the path, he'd seen the trouble banana skins had caused in countless cartoons, they were lethal underfoot) and stood and continued his journey.

Back at Brook Gardens the conversation through the door was continuing, the roles had reversed, Jess was the angry one with the strong words and stoic emotions, Dean was the submissive guilty party pleading for another chance. Cath could sense that eventually Dean's temper would get the better of him and was urging Jess to phone the police, but Jess was having none of it, she was overcoming her fear of Dean and strengthening herself in the process, she had to do this alone.
"Jess, please, this is something we can fix together, I just need your help. I know I made a huge mistake, a massive mistake but it can be fixed."
"No. No more chances Dean, it's done, I want you to leave." Jess returned.
Dean sighed and looked at his feet. This wasn't how he imagined it would go, in his mind Jess understood and would give him one more chance, just one more would do it, Dean wasn't like this, it was a misunderstanding, that's all, how could he expect to fix this if she wouldn't even open the door? Was she crazy? Didn't she see that this wouldn't ever be put right if she didn't let him try? She's lost the plot, completely lost sight of what is best for her, I bet those neighbours have been whispering in her ear, whisper, whisper, whisper, those snidey, poisonous opinions. They never liked him,

they were jealous and never wanted her and Dean to succeed, they were all hung up on Brian, perfect fucking Brian with his software writing, stay-at-home bullshit. Well he wasn't perfect, he moved to Canada when something better came along, leaving Jess and poor Toby on their own. It's his fault. All of this is Brian's fault. He did a job on her alright, they all believed his rubbish. Well screw them, screw all of them, Brian, the new woman, the neighbours, Toby, Jess, yes screw Jess the most, if she's that stupid that she believes it all then he's better off out of it.

But he's not going without his things, that's theft, Dean isn't going without what's his.

"I want me stuff back." He said through the door.

By now a small group of people were watching from their windows, there was obviously something going on at number nineteen, this was better than watching old comedy repeats on BBC One. It looks like the boyfriend has been kicked out.

"Let's talk on the phone later and we'll work out when you can get it" Jess replied.

"No. We can do it now, I'm right here."

Cath took Jess's arm, "Jess, call the police, he's getting angry, call the police".

Jess turned back to the door, "No, call later. Now go away."

"It's my house too!" Dean shouted. He kicked the bottom of the door and it shook; the sound echoed indoors. The monster was at the door and it was going nowhere.

If anybody had the sense to look up the road at this moment, they would have seen a police car innocently driving towards them, the driver inside was counting down the numbers as they passed the different doors, "twenty seven, twenty five, twenty three, twenty one, nine – oh, will you look at this?" Craig said to Emma.

"Looks like the party has already started" she replied concerned.

The police car parked outside number twenty-one and both officers got out, Dean didn't hear either car door close, Emma took a wide route to the neighbouring house but Craig walked directly, taking the shortest route.

"Hello sir - Emma said – misplaced your keys?"
Dean turned and saw Craig and Emma moving towards him.
He's a big lad, Craig thought to himself, he'd take some stopping if he was angry.
"Is everything ok here sir?" Craig asked.
"None of your fucking business" Dean replied and kicked the door again.
Craig could see Emma gesturing to somebody inside the house, he looked and could see an elderly lady looking out of the window.
"How about you come away from the door sir and we'll talk about it, I imagine a big fella like you would be frightening to that lady inside."
Craig guessed the woman was Toby's neighbour, he'd said there were an elderly couple next door. He couldn't see Toby's mum though.
"I said it was none of your business – Dean kicked the door again and shouted at it – I suppose you called the police you fucking bitch!"
"No one called, we heard you shouting from a mile away" Emma said.
"Come away from the door sir." Craig didn't like this man, he knew he had to stay impartial in all cases, not everything is black and white, but seeing him reinforced everything Toby had told them. He must be inside too, probably upstairs in his room petrified.
"Come and make me pig" Dean hissed.
"I don't think I want to. If I have to, I will, but it won't be fun for either of us." Craig said.
Emma was using her radio and requesting backup.
"I'll fight you." Dean called.
"I was told you preferred fighting women and their young sons anyway, I might be more than you can handle sir" Craig smiled.
Dean ran at Craig and grabbed the police vest. Those vests are great for carrying various things but in an altercation, they can be a hindrance. Craig spun and moved Dean off balance, he pushed him and Dean fell to the ground, his knees skidding across the lawn.
The front door opened and Jess and Cath tentatively came out, they stood on the front step without an inch between them.

Dean looked up and gave Jess a look of such hatred that she felt it in her bones, he hated her, he really hated her, his hatred was lava burning through his entire body. He'd lost it, his hands were shaking, his breathing was fast, adrenalin was coursing through him and he bubbled with rage and fury.

On all fours, like an animal, Dean sprang up and lunged at Craig, Craig stepped to one side and kicked Dean in the knee, Dean cried out and dropped down.

Emma looked around and saw a brand-new black Vauxhall Corsa park up a few metres from her, she fronted up not knowing who this was. A man and a woman exited the car and stared at the drama on the front lawn open mouthed.

Emma approached the couple and they introduced themselves, "My name is Brian, this is my fiancé Celia, I used to live here, that is my ex-wife, I had a call from my son Toby to come home. So here I am"

Jess saw Brian and ran to him, Brian embraced her and asked her what was going on (not an unsurprising question considering there was a fight on his old front lawn).

Brian had caught the first flight from Vancouver to Birmingham airport, they travelled overnight and hired a car to take them the rest of the way from Birmingham to Bristol, Celia had searched for hire cars in the terminal in Vancouver and had selected the Vauxhall Corsa, it was the best deal, they could have had a Volkswagen Polo or a Citroen of some description but Celia is a prudent sort, so the Corsa was selected.

Craig urged Dean to come at him again, Craig was more used to tackling people than Dean was and he was more of an equal opponent than Jess or Toby. Craig's glare was unwavering and he would have liked nothing more than to remove his police uniform and take Dean on one-on-one but this wasn't the time.

Craig approached Dean cautiously and read him his rights while he clicked the handcuffs onto Deans wrists. Face down in the lawn, Dean didn't look so frightening to Jess, she almost felt sorry for him, it was clear he had some issues with anger and jealousy, actually the list was much longer than that but Jess no longer cared enough to think about it. It was quite fitting that he ended up laying in the mud. The police van finally arrived and Dean was charged with assaulting a police officer and causing affray, Emma would speak to Jess, she was certain that she could expand those charges to include domestic violence and child abuse.

Craig assisted the hobbling Dean to the car. As they passed Brian said "I assume this is Dean?" Jess nodded and looked ashamed. Brian kissed Jess on the forehead and held her, Celia put her hand on Jess's back and introduced herself to Cath.

"Hang on Jess" Brian said gently, he stepped away from Jess and said "Dean!" as Dean turned Brian punched him full in the mouth, Dean's head shot back and something white and pebble-sized launched from Dean's mouth and landed in the grass.

No further action was taken for Brian assaulting Dean, no one admitted having seen it and it was an unexplained mystery that, over time, became blurred by gossip and Chinese whispers. Nobody bothered to retrieve Dean's ejected tooth, Emma accidentally trod on it, which only pushed it further down into the soil, it's probably still there lying beneath the grass roots of the front lawn of nineteen Brook Gardens.

Chapter Fifteen – Beneath the Stars

There was a certain bitter-sweet atmosphere surrounding the reuniting of Brian and Jess, they'd shared the house for a few years before Toby came along and it felt strange for Brian to be here once again in his old home but with his new fiancé, it felt like Celia shouldn't be there to see the monument of his previous life.
The road was alive with drama and people coming and going, curtains twitched, dogs needed to be suddenly walked immediately and those braver neighbours stood by their front gates and looked on. Younger people took photos and uploaded them to their social media pages, pretty soon the fight at Brook Gardens had gone half way around the world and some photos had gathered over a thousand 'likes'. This was way more likes than Dean would ever get in his life, if only someone took the time to tell him that him being put into a police van was the most watched video the local area had seen since Dolly the African Grey had said "feck off" in a convincing Irish accent to the visiting Jehovah Witnesses.
Just as final statements were being taken and endless cups of tea were being handed around, a red Mazda pulled into the road and parked up near the gathered police cars. A medium sized man dressed in a white shirt with black shoulder tags and black tie exited and looked at the onlookers, with a mixture of puzzlement and embarrassment, he nodded to a few neighbours and made his way to the rear of the car. He opened the boot, pulled out a little suitcase, put it on the ground, extended the handle and dragged it along on its tiny black wheels. He locked the car and walked into the garden of number seventeen.
Jess, Brian, Celia, Cath and Emma all watched the man as he walked up to his front door, entered the key and went in.
"Our neighbour…" said Jess, almost in a dream.
"Was he wearing a pilot's uniform?" Brian looked at Celia.
"I think he was" added Cath.
"I don't get it, what's the problem?" Celia asked.
"I think that's the first time I've ever seen him" Jess looked at Brian.

Another mystery solved, their neighbour, the one once labelled as anything from a drug dealer to a hired killer was an aircraft pilot, admittedly the other scenarios are far more interesting and noteworthy but often the most satisfying result is the dullest and benign.

"Another thing Jim has missed" Cath added, it was typical of Jim to miss the action, he was the kind of man that would go to a football match to find himself standing at the urinal in the toilet when the only goal is scored.

He'd be annoyed to not only have missed Dean get arrested but miss the punch that will go down in folklore as the one that finally vanquished the foe. No amount of descriptive words will make up for that, maybe he can trawl YouTube later for it. No doubt someone managed to catch it.

Jess invited Brian and Celia in for a drink and a catch up, for too long she kept it all to herself, she silently thanked her brave son and made sure to give him a special treat when he came home later.

Brian had so many questions, he looked at the cupboard under the stairs and tried not to think about how many times his son was thrown in there, Celia almost read his mind and touched his arm, she quietly said "not now", she understood Jess was going through a healing process too, much had happened in a short space of time and Brian hadn't slept very much over the last twenty four hours, the best thing to do was be kind. Questions and accusations can wait. Cath had already reassured Brian that Toby was safe and wasn't a part of what had just happened, he was at the garden centre with Jim, and would be home any minute. Brian was partly thankful for that; he didn't want Toby anywhere near all of this but a selfish part of him wished he had seen him punch Dean in the face. Violence never solved anything, or so people like to say, but Brian was proud of his reaction and it wouldn't do his street cred any harm if Toby had seen it.

Once the kettle was boiled for the umpteenth time and yet more biscuits were handed around, Jim's car turned into next doors drive, Cath went to the front door to beckon he and Toby in.

From the lounge Jess could hear something was wrong, Toby had pricked himself on a rose plant at the garden centre was her initial thought, Brian was seconds behind Cath, he couldn't wait to see Toby again.

Cath returned to the lounge with a look of fear on her face, "Jess, Toby wasn't with Jim!"

Jess stood and her question of "what?" was etched on her face.

Toby had covered a few more miles, it was hard going for his short legs and he had to keep looking at the map and using his compass whenever he reached a road crossing, the plan of climbing hills and then riding them back down again was a fallacy, it wasn't happening yet, the terrain was relatively flat and, on the occasion he had to climb a small incline it wouldn't be enough to ride down the other side so he had no choice other than to walk down with the cart handle bashing against his back side.

He knew it was lunchtime, his stomach had a built-in alarm that informed him, and it seemed every pub had Sunday roast on the menu and the scent of cooked meat and vegetables on the wind. But he was determined, what was the point in risking so much only to turn around once he grew hungry? He kept going, following roads with paths and, if the path for some reason stopped, he would look for a way into the adjoining field and walk the other side of the hedgerow. Every so often he would stoop down and pick up small sticks, he was rather excited at the prospect of building and lighting a fire, the man on the television said it was a great way to keep motivated and keep your spirits up if they begin to dwindle. Toby knew this journey was going to be difficult, and he knew at some point his 'spirit' would drop, so he thought it a good idea to collect fire wood as and when he saw it.

He was told that another way of keeping positive was to sing, apparently singing boosted your happy genes and could make even the grumpiest of grumpy people smile, but Toby's voice wasn't very good and he wasn't much of a music lover. He would have to light a fire.

He had passed a few pieces of pizza thoughtlessly rejected in a box on a bench so he put that in his cart, he would have liked some drink to go with it but the only drinks he came across were empty plastic bottles of cola or other fizzy drinks, he saw a few bottles with a yellow fluid inside, he hoped it wasn't what he thought it was. He gave these a wide berth.

Before long he had gone past the last pieces of the world he recognised, this was all new to him, the great wide world was stretched before him like an empty book, ready for him to write page after page of his wonderous adventures and thoughts. He stopped near a sign for a place called Maidenhead and bit into a piece of cold, stale pizza, it was delicious, so delicious in fact that he had a second and third bite until the slice was gone, he even ate the crust. He'd heard people at school moan about the pizza crust, they said it was dry and horrible, like a hard piece of wood, Toby thought it was ok, he munched it down like it was his last meal. He wished he had saved up all of his friend's pizza crusts, they would have been heavy to pull in his cart but it would have solved one of his big problems of how he was going to eat on this trip.

He was certain he could eat a bird or rabbit; he knew he could cook it on the fire ok, but how do you go about catching one? He knew a little about traps but traps took time to build and they really only worked if you were staying in one place for a while in a camp, Toby was constantly moving. He gave it some thought as he picked up another stick and threw it in the cart.

"What do you mean he wasn't with you?!" Jess screamed.
"He didn't come with me, he hadn't asked me, I had no idea he was coming" Jim replied, the feeling in the room had gone from some level of normality to panic, not one person was thinking correctly or sensibly. Cath had some hair-brained idea that somehow Dean had got Toby, obviously she kept this to herself but it took a few seconds before her mind told her how stupid that was. Jim wondered if Toby was locked in his shed, it would be a nice outcome, of course Toby would be a little miffed but being locked in the shed while all this

commotion was going on, but it's better than the thought of him being somewhere else.

Brian and Celia were playing catch up, they were busy trying to keep up with everything that had happened since they landed earlier this morning, they needed sleep and, in a few hours' time they would be useless to anybody.

"Well he can't be far; I know it's silly but is he in his room? Maybe he hid when Dean turned up" Brian offered.

"Dean turned up?!" Jim asked shocked.

"Yes Jim, Dean was here, try to keep up" Cath barked at him.

"Well I wasn't to know, what happened, where is he now?" Jim was looking around the room as if they'd stowed him away beneath the sofa.

"He scuffled with your police and Brian punched him in the face" Celia added.

"Oh my God, there was a fight? Brian hit him – Jim turned to Brian and patted him on the shoulder – good for you son, glad somebody did. Hang on – he looked at Celia – who are you? Have we met?"

Celia stood and walked to Jim with her hand out "I'm Celia, Brian's other woman", Jim shook her hand and looked at Jess as the words sunk in, "Oh, well, um I guess it's nice to meet you".

"Don't worry Jim, Celia's alright, she brought Brian home, which is good enough for me" Jess said.

"Um, it still doesn't solve where my son is" Brian shouted.

"*Our* son!" Jess replied just as loud.

"Oh, you know what I mean" Brian said immediately calming down.

"I'll check his room" Cath said making for the stairs.

"I'll see if he's in our garden or shed, you hear cats getting locked in sheds all the time" he muttered as he walked out of the back door.

"I'll come with you" Brian said.

Jess grabbed the tea mugs and looked at Celia, who was standing awkwardly in the middle of the room, "I'm sure he'll be fine" she said with more confidence than she believed.

A few seconds passed before Cath called down, "nothing". Jess, in some perverse train of thought checked in the cupboard under the stairs, she closed the door feeling ashamed at what that cupboard had been recently used for. It used to be the dumping ground for suitcases and the occasional cheap bottle of wine, now it had taken on a new meaning, the police will want to photograph it no doubt for their case building, they'll need to photograph lots of things... hang on, the police!

Jess scrambled to the table, Jim and Brian returned, it was clear from their faces they'd found nothing, "Jim says his cart is missing from his shed, he reckons Toby used to play with – what are you doing?" Jess picked up the card one of the police officers had left, "Craig Farr, I'll call him, he seemed to know a lot about Toby – she looked at the others in the room – he was the one who arrested Dean. He asked where Toby was before he left, I think he knew him."

"Do you think he's run away?" Celia asked.

No one had had this thought before, Toby was just missing, no, no he wasn't *missing*, that's the wrong word, that suggests he's run off somewhere and Toby wasn't the sort of child to run off. Not without his mum anyway. Dean did a lot of damage but Toby wouldn't leave his mum alone to cope with this. Toby wouldn't run away, he was just out somewhere, but the truth was he was only seven years old (nearly eight) and it wasn't safe for a child of that age to be out on his own.

Toby was making good time on his walk, the weather was on his side, it was bright but cool and he had found a rhythm with his cart that made moving seem easy. Of course, he had moments where his mind drifted off and he would think of random things like do you get male pigs or are they all females? Or, do pirates still exist? And where do frogs go when it gets cold? These thoughts tormented and distracted him as one foot went in front of the other over and over and over and over again. Pretty soon he was making his way through villages and quiet pathways, high hedges gave him protection from cars as he walked along the other side out of view, he was still picking up small sticks and looking out for things he could eat. He knew his stock of food and water from the shop wouldn't last him the entire journey so he began to eat only when hungry and he was careful not to be greedy. He would have given all of his money for some tomato ketchup but he tried not to think about that.

He came to a village called Dundry, he could see on the map that there was a hill that he didn't really want to travel over. The cart seemed to increase in weight whenever a hill presented itself, he had already tackled one and he had to rest for a few moments before carrying on. He thought about sitting and trying to sing to feel a little happier but he concluded it might draw attention to him and the last thing a cyclist or rambler expects to stumble across is a young boy lying flat on his back singing the words from a Disney film or radio jingle. No, he kept quiet and chose his steps carefully.

Travelling through the village was easy enough, he blended in with the locals and tourists, there were people riding on bikes, people chatting on the pavements and more dogs than he had ever seen before. Near the church was something that caught his eye, an inn. Toby had begun to think of inn's and pubs as possible feeding grounds, he needed to think of himself as something of a scavenger, he was a swooping magpie, a courageous pigeon, if he wanted to eat without breaking into his money, these were the places to visit. There were no signs for fast food outlets, pubs and inns would have to do.

It took timing, luck and the heart of a lion to successfully get food. Toby approached the front of the pub, there were a few tables out front, each with plates of uneaten food on them, mostly chips and the occasional half a sausage or garlic bread but there was also an oval ceramic bowl half-full of lasagne, this would be the gold medal, Toby could taste the pasta and tomato sauce already. But how to get it...

He sat on a bench near the table and rifled through his belongings, considering the day he had had the cart was still well organised, Harold had been doing his job really well, he'd kept a clean cart. Well done Harold.

One of the women on a nearby table noticed him and smiled, she then looked around him for his guardian or parent. Toby wondered if she was going to say anything, but she didn't, she just carried on talking. Toby noticed a small sign on the pub door that told people to take a seat, note the table number and please order their food at the bar. It didn't take him long to come up with an idea. He walked to the table with the food on, sat down, got himself comfortable and sat like he owned the world. He suddenly looked at the pubs open door and said "pardon?", obviously there was no reply, no one was stood there, but Toby carried on, "oh – he looked for the table number and looked back at the door – it's number seventeen. Shall I clear the plates mum?"

He nodded and started gathering up all of the food, he scraped the food onto one plate and left it on the table, the empty plates he stacked up and carried them into the pub, on his way he looked at the lady who had noticed him and asked, "Could you watch my cart for me while I take this in please?" The lady nodded and replied of course, what a polite young boy, clearing the table so his mum had somewhere to put their food.

Toby entered the pub, put the plates on the first table he found and started back out, on his way he passed a small rack of knives, forks, spoons and all manner of condiments, there were sachets of salt, pepper, sugar, sweetener and little plastic pouches of sauces. Mustard, salad cream, brown sauce, mayonnaise, something called tartare with a picture of a fish on it and, there it was, tomato ketchup.

Toby acted natural and helped himself to some napkins, knives, fork, spoons, sugar and a handful of ketchup. He exited the pub, thanked the lady for watching his cart and sat back down. The food was so close, he wanted to scoff the food down right there and then, but he couldn't, instead he turned to the door and said "Pardon, what? Why? – he looked around the garden – well I guess we could, if you wanted... ok" he got up from his table and walked to another behind the woman, he then returned to the door, "It's number twenty one then, I'll move our stuff" he grabbed the handle of his cart, put the plate of food into it and walked off to another table. He didn't stop, he kept on walking, down the road near the church and off to tackle this hill. He would be eating lasagne, chips and garlic bread for dinner tonight, as he trundled off with the cart rattling behind him, he took a bite of the half-sausage and smiled. All he would need is an endless supply of pubs and he could eat like a king at Christmas.

"They said officer Farr has finished for the day but he'll be back tomorrow, they asked if I wanted to leave a message, maybe I should have but Toby's only been out for a few hours" Jess was at odds with what to do, something was telling her that something was wrong, Toby liked to go out and she had suspected he used to go further than what she told him, one day she went as far as to follow him, he went all the way to the big shop. It was all she could do to drag him back but she also realised he was getting older now and he was a sensible child, he pressed the button for the traffic lights, waited for the green man to inform him when it was safe to cross, and he didn't get into any harm. He was a resourceful child and seemed to recognise good in people, he steered clear of the trouble makers at school but also had the air about him that told potential bullies to keep away. He was doing well at school, he wasn't a child prodigy or anything like that, and he preferred the outdoors to stuffy classrooms but he was a good student, he was above where he should be at his age with regards to his studies. But something nagged at her, he should be home, he rushed his breakfast, she thought at the time his cereal bowl was practically still spinning as he left the house. He also missed lunch, this never happened. She thought maybe he returned a little after Dean and ran off to somewhere he felt safe but she had no idea where that could be, could he have come back during the scuffle? Would she have noticed him if he had? Her attention was on the police officer and Dean, and then Brian returning made her head spin even more, actually the more she thought about it, the more she felt like she was in a film or, even worse, a dream and she would wake up lying next to a snoring Dean.
"He hasn't been gone long Jess – Cath offered – maybe we should try and stay calm" it was nearly three in the afternoon and no one would

organise a search party after such a short time. He could be sat in a cinema tucking into a bucket of popcorn somewhere for all they knew.

"If Toby had decided to go somewhere else, where would he go?" Brian asked.

"I'm not sure, he loves being outdoors, maybe he's gone to the park, but he wouldn't go by himself" Jess walked to the kitchen and checked the cupboards for missing food.

"What are you checking?" Jim said.

"I was wondering if he had taken any food to eat, but it all seems ok, there are a few things missing, crisps, peanuts, maybe some bread but not loads of things – she opened the cupboard beneath the sink – his water bottle for school has gone" she said.

"Could it be in his room with his bag?" Cath asked. She had checked his room but she didn't notice if his school bag was missing.

"I'll check" she turned to go.

"No, no, I'll check - Brian put up a hand and walked up the stairs to his room, going the wrong way, he turned and called down – Toby went into the small room?"

"Yes, Dean keeps, sorry, *kept* his stuff in the bigger room, Toby moved into your old office" she called.

"I can't see his bag" he called down.

As he entered the room with the others he added, "I couldn't see it. What are you thinking?"

"I don't know but it doesn't make sense." Jess's eyes raced around as her mind went through one scenario after another.

"I don't want to sound dramatic but do you think he might have had enough and run away?" Jim's question was met with an array of facial expressions but all eyes fell on Jess.

"No, I don't think so. This doesn't feel right, but I can't understand why he would go. I wonder if he's at a friend's house, maybe a friend I haven't met yet, and time has gotten away from him"

"Could he have told you but you'd forgotten? Maybe forgot to write it down?" Celia asked.

"Why would he say he was going with me though?" Jim added.

"Yes -Cath chimed in – he said he was going with Jim to the garden centre"
Jess looked at her ex-husband, she realised her life had fallen apart after he had left, some bad choices had led to this; their only child missing.
"I'm calling that police man again and getting a message to him, this isn't right." She picked up the phone and dialled the number.

The view was something quite special, for miles around the landscape spread out and opened like a painting. On any other occasion Toby would have breathed in the view like he was breathing in the fresh air, but he was too busy pulling his cart through the knee-high grass, following a pathway that had been trodden into the ground by a thousand feet. It was a bumpy trek and made more difficult by excitable dogs who, more than once, gave a playful glance towards Harold at the rear of the cart. Toby had promised himself a well-earnt rest at the foot of the hill, he had filled his water bottle from an outdoor tap in someone's front garden before he started so he had drink, food and a place to sleep, the question was where would he find a suitable place to park the cart so he wouldn't be disturbed. From the map he realised Bristol Airport was nearby, the last thing he needed was some nosey passenger looking out of the window and seeing him asleep in his cart. He wondered if people could see him or if the airplane would be too high or going too fast, it made him wonder if, when the time came, and he needed to visit the toilet, would it be a good idea to put the umbrella up so nobody from above could spy down on him doing his business. This thought kept his mind busy as he trod through the long grass and finally made his way down the other side.
It was getting late, if he was back home it would be his bath time, he could picture his mum running the water and putting the washing away, there was a time when that would be the norm, but too soon that image was given the added inclusion of Dean watching television downstairs.

Toby thought about the letter he wrote his mum, he hoped she read it and wouldn't be mad at him, but she shouldn't be, he was giving her a way out, he knew Dean didn't make her happy, with any luck his mum was packing her suitcases and ordering Dean to empty that blasted spare room and get out.
He tried not to think of his mum too much, it made him sad because although he was now an intrepid explorer, he still missed her.

There was a knock at the door and Celia, who had quickly become a part of this team of misfits, opened it. Standing there was a man in his thirties wearing a blue hoodie, jeans, running shoes and holding a dog lead. On the other end of the lead was, unsurprisingly, a dog. Celia noted how the expressions on the faces were in stark contrast, the man looked concerned and ready for action while the dog seemed simply happy to be out. The man introduced himself as police officer Farr, Celia knew this already, she remembered him from earlier on, she didn't think she would ever forget what had happened that day and, in truth, the drama didn't look like stopping anytime soon.
Celia stepped to the side and invited them both in, she looked at Lizzie and wondered if the dog had any idea what was going on or it was just happy to be somewhere new where the smells would trigger excitement. Dogs seem to have such a simple life, Celia grew up in a house of dogs, her parents loved having at least two dogs around and it made for an interesting childhood. Celia, being the youngest of three children, had two brothers that grew up loving the outdoors. Regular walks and camping trips were the order of the day and being surrounded by two adults, two dogs and two older brothers, she was nothing if not well protected. Canada is a tempting landscape for hikers and campers, with dense forests and vast landscape that offers something new with each coming season. Growing up in a country shared with bears makes a person understand their place in the pecking order, you might think you're a big shot while you wander the pathways carrying a rifle but, at the end of the day, you're only as good as the forest allows you to be, there are plenty of

things a rifle doesn't protect you from. Celia's childhood was one of a good diet, good morals and always feeling part of something bigger, her parents never allowed her to forget how fragile life was and how much work you should put into happiness because it can so easily and quickly go.

Her feelings for Brian came as something of a shock to her and she was constantly in the grip of conflict, Brian was married and had fostered a young boy, Celia's introduction was something that wasn't planned or required, she knew her conversations with her company's software designer was going down a path that would eventually lead to a difficult decision but love is addictive and almost impossible to fight.

One thing she was always certain about, and it was something she remained unmoved on, was she would never be the other woman, she was not about to allow a man to cheat on their wife, if - and it was a big if - Brian was serious about giving up his life with his wife in England, he had to leave her. Of course, she wasn't so heartless that she expected – or wanted - him to say goodbye to his son, but it needed to be as clean as it could be.

When she told her oldest brother, Terrence is his name, about Brian, he shook his head and teased her that she'd been single for a few years and had taken to stealing other women's husband's, she was offended at the suggestion and quickly informed him that that wasn't the case at all. Terrence, for a six foot plus Canadian hulk of a man, also has the sensibility of a best friend and could see this Englishman was different, he meant something more to his baby sister than all those who had come before. He advised her to keep a little distance but to also go after what she wanted, but to also keep this from their parents. Their parents were old fashioned and wanted the best for their only daughter, they would have ideally had her married off years before to a promising young doctor or maybe an architect who would eventually design and build a one-off home in the forest miles from Vancouver but just close enough for the family to visit at weekends or for celebrations (like the news of a grandchild or three?).

All in all, things had worked out for the best and, considering how the relationship began, they now found themselves engaged to be married and the family have accepted the software designer as one of the family. So what if he doesn't like ice hockey or camping in the woods, the English are famously reserved, they've seen the way he treats Celia and it's clear she loves him.

"So how long has he been missing?" Craig asked as he's handed a cup of tea.

"The last time I saw him was around ten this morning" Jess said.

"We've tried coming up with logical answers but nothing really fits" Brain added.

"Yeah, it doesn't sound like him, obviously I'm no expert but he doesn't seem to be the sort of kid to stay away from home for long" Craig started writing things in his book. Some of the people in the room craned their necks to read it in the hope it was something insightful and ground-breaking but all it read was; Missing since 10am.

"Well the questions we would ask are 'could he be at a friend's house?', 'could he just be out and has forgotten to call?' or 'do you have any idea where he could have gone?' but I'm assuming you've been through these already?" Craig asked.

"This is totally out of character for him" Cath said.

"Does he have a special place that he likes to run off to? Something like a favourite park? You'd be amazed at how many children we find asleep at the park."

The whole room shook their heads, Lizzie took this as a sign that this was a good time to sit down and lick her paw, it was going to be a long night and there wasn't very much worth sniffing or eating.

"He asked me to print out a map yesterday – offered Jim – I printed it but he didn't take it."

"A map?" Jess and Cath spoke at the same time.

"Yes, he wanted to know where Weston-Super-Mare was and how to get there."

"You've only thought to say this now?" Cath said, mentally rolling up her sleeves for a fight.

"Well, it didn't seem important, he doesn't have the map, it's at home" Jim quickly added.

"So where is the map now?" Craig asked, writing something in his book again.

"Well it's at home, it's on the recycling pile, I didn't throw it out in case he changed his mind"

"Well go get it! - Cath barked, she then turned to Jess – I'm so sorry Jess, he's losing his marbles, I said before he forgets things"

Jim rose from a chair and made his way to the back door.

Brian stood silent in the corner, he was deep in thought, something about the shed.

"The garden cart was missing" he said to nobody in particular.

"Sorry, what?" Jess replied.

"Yes, when Jim and I checked the shed – he looked at Craig – we checked in case Toby had locked himself in there by accident, Jim said something about a cart not being there."

Suddenly things seemed to be making sense, had Toby runaway and had taken the cart with him? He wouldn't get far because he'd left the map, but that didn't reassure Jess at all, she knew Toby could read a basic map, he would no doubt be armed with Brian's compass, but no map meant her son was lost.

She ran upstairs.

"The compass" she said as she took the stairs two at a time.

The group heard her enter Toby's room and she was rummaging around his bed, "it's gone – she called down – his compass has gone!"

Craig wrote in his book.

Jim re-entered the kitchen holding the paper, "Jess? – he called – you need to see this, it's not a map, it's a letter from Toby"

Jess raced down the stairs, her mind was scrambled, so many thoughts, so many questions and no clear answer. She grasped the paper and stood in the centre of the lounge reading it, all eyes were on Jess's as they moved from side to side reading her son's scratchily pencilled words. She stopped reading.

"He's gone to Weston-Super-Mare to find us a nicer place to live."

Craig stood up and said he'd call the station and get them to call the Weston police, he'd need a recent photo and a description and they'd start looking immediately, he was trying to put their minds at rest but they all knew he wouldn't be there yet, he was seven (nearly eight) but he was also dragging a cart filled with God knows what and he wouldn't make much ground.
Craig left the room and started talking into his mobile phone.
Cath punched Jim in the arm but also kissed him on the cheek.
Brian hugged Jess and suggested they look at what exactly was missing from his room, it was nearing eight o'clock in the evening and normally Toby would be in bed by now, wherever he was he would be tired, afraid and alone, there was no idea what kind of danger he was in.

Toby was sitting on a square of polystyrene with his legs crossed and was drinking water from his bottle and watching the planes fly over. He couldn't remember the last time he was this content. The lasagne had been polished off and he tucked into a biscuit as he looked at the map in front of him. His mum would have loved this, there was no Dean, no washing up to do and, apart from the aeroplanes, little or no noise, occasionally he heard a bird swooping across the sky on its way back to its nest but he was happy enough. He kept his wind-up torch close by, it wasn't dark yet but the light wasn't penetrating the little clump of trees that he found himself in.
Tomorrow he would need to find more sticks for the fire, he had used over half of his supply but the glow and warmth was worth it. As he climbed into his sleeping bag and curled up in the cart with Harold tucked under his chin, he started thinking of the following day's journey, he would be moving closer to the airport so would need to be more careful.
With that thought, and a few mouthfuls of air, he was falling asleep.

Chapter Sixteen – Another Canada

Craig had a map laid out on the kitchen table, he drew a circle from Brook Gardens, "so we're here, going by what the station said, Toby will only cover a few miles in the time that he's been missing, which means he's still in Bristol" he looked up at the group.

Celia was asleep on the sofa finally having succumb to the length of time she's been awake, Brian was sitting in the lounge nearby, head lolling as he fought sleep, Cath was stood wrapped in one of Jess's cardigans while Jess and Jim listened intently to Craig. Emma, who had turned up a little earlier, was in the kitchen surrounded by empty mugs and glasses speaking on the phone.

"Our best bet is to let the police do their job and see what happens in the morning, I'll call in some favours, Em is already calling our colleagues to tell them to keep an eye out, but not much will be done, officially, until tomorrow."

Jess laughed at this, she'd be damned if she would make a mug of cocoa and simply go to bed as if nothing had happened, her son was out in the dark. It was all her fault she thought, if only she had stood up to Dean (which made her remember the time she did, she ended up asleep in Toby's room with a sore chest and more fear than she had ever felt) if only she had realised what was going on sooner, why didn't she see Jim to make sure Toby was going with him? That was another thing that made no sense, did Toby ever intend to go with Jim?

Emma said that he probably did and he was going to maybe use it as a lift to get him closer to his destination, but luckily it had backfired. Who knows where he would be now if he'd left Jim at the garden centre?

"I'm guessing he's travelled about three or four miles – said Craig – considering his age, fitness, the fact he's dragging the cart and depending on direction. The map suggests south west, so he'll be near Whitchurch, I say we start there – he looks at Emma – Whitchurch?"

Emma nods and relays the word 'Whitchurch' down the phone.

"We'll start at the supermarket and work in a circle from there, for all we know he's sitting on a bench eating an ice cream" Craig writes in his book and makes for the door.
"I'm coming too" Jess says.
Craig stops and looks at her as Emma makes her way past.
"Don't say it, Craig, don't say anything, if you think I'm staying here and drinking more tea, you're mental" Jess said.
"I'm coming too" Jim said looking at Cath.
"More the merrier" Jess said.
"I can't stop you, of course you want to look but what if he comes home?"
Jess looks at Celia and Brian who are fast asleep.
Craig looks too. He sighs.
"Come on then but we'll swap phone numbers so we can keep in touch."

Toby had never heard a fox cry before, to say it scared him would be to underestimate his reaction. It was unnerving and frightening. Toby didn't know what to do, looking up at the pointing fingers of the trees overhead, Toby squeezed his eyes tighter together and started to cry, if Harold was waiting for his moment to shine, then this was it, but what use was a rabbit against whatever monster it was that was howling in the dark. Toby shone his torch over the top of the cart and looked around, he could see the trunks of the nearest trees but the torch beam couldn't reach much further into the woods and the light was eaten up. Toby took the umbrella and put it up, laying it in the cart it sat lopsided and awkward but it offered a little more shelter that made Toby feel slightly better.
Toby looked out again and saw the brown fur of a fox, his torch shone down the length of the animal before it ran back into the woods.
"Hello mister Fox - Toby whispered – you keep away from here, I don't have any food for you" Toby looked into the darkness until he fell asleep again, he breathed deeply and dreamt of nothing as his

hair was moved by the summer breeze and the world slowly moved from dark to dawn.

Toby was awake and eating a banana before it was fully light, at some point during the night he had the idea of getting an early start and trying to get past the airport before it got busy. His mum had called it 'rush hour' and it was when everyone chose to drive their cars, why someone would want to drive their car really slow didn't make sense to Toby, but he knew it meant the roads were busy so the best way to avoid the added attention was to go now. He kicked dirt onto the fire, it had gone out hours before but he'd seen his television man do it, so maybe he should to.
He crossed a busy road and made his way past the airport, it was slow going, he decided to drink and walk instead of stopping for a rest but his feet soon started to ache, he looked down at his feet and decided to count his steps, maybe this would take his mind off the distance he had to travel. His map was so big and it didn't seem like he was ticking off the villages as fast as he would have liked, he visited a place called Redhill which confused him because it wasn't red at all, he wondered this as he travelled up and down it. He was looking forward to seeing a red hill, maybe it would have those vivid red flowers like the ones people wear in the autumn for the soldiers but he didn't see any, maybe it was the wrong time of year.
Upon leaving Redhill Toby was finally able to use the cart as a vehicle, it was time for the cart to repay Toby for dragging it all this way. The road was downhill for quite some time so Toby put one foot in the cart and the other outside and he used it as an over-sized scooter, he went a little faster than he would have chosen but it was difficult to control and even more difficult to slow down. He was able to steer relatively well and he was able to make up a large distance in a short time. He found a certain happiness in learning the road he was travelling on was called Long Lane because, even to this seven-year-old, it *was* a long lane. This was the highlight of the trip so far, even Harold looked like he was smiling, no mean feat to a rabbit that spends most of his time tucked away in a room.

Slowing down he saw signs for a pub a few hundred metres ahead, he didn't really know how far that was but he knew it wasn't far, and just in time, breakfast had come and gone, so too had most of his stock of food, he needed to replenish his energy and his food reserves, he hoped they were busy so he could recycle the unwanted food. He had money to buy things but he wasn't sure how much food at a pub would cost and he didn't know when he would really need to spend it.

Overnight, the mood was a dreary and tiring exercise in looking for a needle in a haystack, no one had seen anything and it proved fruitless in asking passers-by or people out for a walk. Sunday quickly turned into Monday and already thoughts of never seeing Toby again entered everybody's minds.
The one saving grace was they knew where he was going, if they were patient, they could sit on the beach front, tuck into some fish and chips and wait until Toby simply turned up. They all knew he would eventually, he was resourceful, intelligent, knew more than any of them about finding water, heat and shelter, but the simple fact was, he was a young boy and who knew the amount of dangers out in the wide world there was for a trusting seven-year-old. It didn't bear thinking about, and most of the search party fought away such thoughts. He would turn up safe and sound, they just needed to look in the correct place.
Eventually they returned to nineteen Brook Gardens.
Brian and Celia had woken up and Celia was making some food while Brian spoke to Jess on the phone, at first he was angry at not being woken to join the search team but Celia had reminded him that he was tired, he'd have been near to useless and now wasn't the time for blaming others, they needed to stick together and work together, besides, maybe they could go and look while the others rested.
Craig and Emma contacted Weston-Super-Mare police again and asked for an update, but it was a long shot, no way could Toby have reached the coast, not unless he got a lift or caught a bus.

No, the idea was ridiculous, he was still in Bristol, he would have gotten tired and found a quiet place to sleep. Craig drove to cemeteries in the area and Emma went to parks, both were relatively quiet at night and make nice places to sleep, if you're not a believer in ghosts that is and Toby didn't seem the sort to worry about ghosts or zombies, he's only young, he wouldn't even know what a zombie was, let alone be able to recognise one.

Things were going well for Toby, he was now the proud owner of two bowls of cold chips, three halves of baguette, a small tub of something resembling coleslaw, another sachet of ketchup, half a pizza and some fish in batter. He'd had to work a little quicker this time, the weather was turning colder and the tables outside the pub were empty but he had to dash to get the food between the visits from the waiting staff. Once someone took a pile of empty plates in, he sprinted and picked up anything he could. He made a special trip for the ketchup; it was worth it. He could eat fish and chips later. Pretty soon he passed a small farm, outside there was a sign saying 'eggs for sale' above a table with dozens of eggs on grey cardboard trays, on the table, taped to the surface was the price list, Toby didn't need six eggs, so he took two and left some money, he wasn't sure how much it would cost for two eggs but he tried to make sure it was more than enough, he popped them in the safe custody of Harold and carried on.

He sat by the road side and started to cut the handle of his umbrella, the rain had begun to fall and the umbrella was too tall, it kept catching the wind and threatening to blow away, so he took out a knife and started sawing away, it was slow going, the knife kept sliding up the aluminium pole, but eventually he cut it down. He laid it over the cart but it was still too tall so he had to cut the base of the cart, he found the knife with the triangular blade was the best for this, it cut it no problem and the umbrella sat nicely on top of the cart. It kept his things dry and when it really began to rain hard, he was able to gather water from it and collect it in his water bottle.

Off he went again, his arms cold from the rain sticking to his rain coat.

He looked at his map, next up was a place called St. George, it was nice to be going to a place that shared its name with his school friend, how perfect, he didn't know there was a place called that, he wondered if there was a St. Toby somewhere, he made a note to ask his mum to put it into the computer, maybe he could walk there, if it wasn't too far of course. He didn't think he could go too far, and England was an island after all, so if it was very far, he'd need to think about packing a boat next time and he didn't think the cart would be big enough.

He soon saw a sign for an animal park, he knew the name of the place, he'd seen little folded paper brochures in the big shop for it, he thought he'd been there before but he couldn't remember, you've seen one giant slide, you've seen them all and he wasn't a fan of ball parks and getting pushed by nine year olds in those places. He remembered holding a baby pig once and thinking how strange it felt and he'd seen pictures of him feeding a small white animal but if it was a lamb or a goat or a polar bear, he wouldn't know (well he knew it wasn't a polar bear, everyone knew what one of those looked like and the chances are if you were feeding it, you were probably feeding it you!), this seemed a good place to stop, he'd made good progress today, he didn't know how far it was but it was probably around one hundred miles, he needed a way of drying out the wood for the fire, that would be considerably more difficult with wet wood, he wasn't sure if he knew how to get a fire started if the wood was wet. He hoped the rain would stop soon; it had been slowing for a little while but he was probably travelling with the rain clouds. But the plan was made, get to the animal park and stop (and hope there aren't many foxes).

"There was a report yesterday of a boy on a bus pulling a trolley" Emma's voice came down the phone like a bolt of luck. Craig had needed some good news, this felt different from the other children he'd attempted to find.

"You're joking? That's great news, hang on I'll put you on speaker so we can all hear" Craig put the phone on the table and gestured for people to come closer.

"A driver picked up a boy from the supermarket near Toby's home yesterday morning, he thought it was odd so he radioed it back, apparently the boy said he was meeting a grandparent along the route to Whitchurch" Emma said.

"Whitchurch? So, he *was* in Whitchurch?" Cath said to Jess.

"What grandparent?" Brian asked.

Craig put his hand up to quieten the group, "Em, did the driver see the grandparent?"

"He didn't say, but maybe there wasn't a grandparent, could Toby have just said that to fool the driver into letting him on board?" Craig looked at Jess with his eyebrows raised.

"I don't know, maybe, but that sounds a little deceitful for Toby" she said.

"I'm waiting on an image from the on-board CCTV, once it's through I'll photograph it and send it across, it should only be a few minutes."

"That's great Em, thanks, keep us posted" Craig clicked the phone to end the call and moved it aside to reveal the map on the table underneath.

"So, he was here yesterday – pointing at the map – we were looking at where he had been, not where he was, he's moved very fast. I'm impressed." Craig looked up with a feeling of pride, he knew that little boy was special.

No one shared his feeling, he received blank looks in response.

"Sorry – he coughed – I just think it's remarkable that he was able to do that"

His phone beeped and he reached for it, he opened an image that Emma had sent through, "It's him".

Jess looked at the phone and passed it around the others, who, in turn, nodded in agreement.

"The little bugger" Jim said without anger.

"He's elusive, isn't he?" Cath said mirroring Jim's sentiment.

"I'm looking forward to meeting him" Celia said. Jess looked at her and gave her a hug. Brian looked at his ex-wife and felt pride for not only knowing two amazing women but also realising they both allowed him to enter their lives.

"We just need to find the little sod" Brian said.

Craig was looking at the map with Jim, making calculations and sharing knowledge on the area Toby was travelling through, it was clear the airport hadn't reported seeing or finding a young boy travelling nearby, so that either meant Toby wasn't there yet, or he has passed there, Jim said the journey from Redhill was mostly downhill so he would make good ground, the cart wasn't suitable for riding like a go-cart but even so, travelling downhill was easier than up.

"St. George is nearby; I wonder if he could reach that before dark?" Craig looked at Jim thoughtfully.

"Do you think so? – Jim replied – but what is he eating? If he was a grown man, I'd say yes, but this is a boy, without food and no real idea where he's going, I think he's somewhere between here – he pointed to the map – and here."

"Yeah, that seems possible. Either way, he'll be needing to stop soon, the weather today will have slowed him down, I say we drive to St. George and work back from there, if he's sticking to the roads, we'll see him, if he's not, he'll lose time and he'll be back towards the airport, if they don't pick him up." Craig turned and phoned Emma.

"Well you heard him, let's get going" Jim said to the group.

Cath had been making sandwiches and preparing flasks of tea, the group were ready.

Along the road was a billboard sign for the animal park, 'fun-packed, all-weather' it boasted, it also boasted a nice area behind the sign where the rain didn't reach, this was the place to stop the cart, it was secluded from the road with high grass and a small hollow in the ground that the cart could nestle in.

The fire took a while to get going but eventually it started producing heat and Toby started to warm up. He put some water into a tin can he found along the way and put his eggs in, he placed it in the centre of the fire and after a few minutes tiny bubbles appeared in the water, his plan was to let them boil, they would make a nice breakfast, he wished he had some bread, butter and an electric toaster but the eggs would have to do.

He heard dozens of cars passing this way and that as he happily tucked into his dinner, he took his shoes off and placed them near the fire to dry and was secretly looking forward to going to bed in his newly-modified cart, complete with roof. He wasn't sure how he would position his body around the metal pole but it would be worth it to stay warm and dry. The rain had ceased but the feeling of damp was still in the air.

He took out the map and smiled at the idea he was travelling to a place with his friend's name, he would set off there early tomorrow. He removed the tin can from the fire with a pair of sticks and set them on the floor near the cart and made himself comfortable beneath the umbrella.

Sleep found him suddenly and without warning, Toby fell into another deep sleep as the day darkened and the cars drove by, among them his mum, dad and the rest of the group passed just metres from him, they travelled too fast to notice the smell of the slowly-dying fire or the sound of a little boy, snoring soundly.

Craig was keeping in contact with his police in Bristol but also kept in regular touch with the Somerset police, he was able to get a bit more help due to him being a policeman and he told those he wasn't familiar with that the boy ran away as a result of the arrest of his mums boyfriend. They were all sympathetic towards Toby, none of them sided with the abusive partner and finding a child from that background was something they all wanted to help with. But news was slow in coming. How could a child simply disappear with no-one seeing him, it simply shouldn't be possible but that was something that helped Toby, unintentionally those who saw Toby couldn't believe he was on his own, surely an adult would be close by and people found comfort in this fact. Boy's didn't go out alone. Toby was able to cover distances without seeing anyone at all, people worked, people were preoccupied or were travelling, once they had seen him, he was just something else in the rear-view mirror, out of sight, out of mind.

It was late when the group arrived in St. George, Craig decided to visit the police station and introduce himself and bring people up to speed, officially he wasn't back at work until Thursday but he wasn't about to let people know that, it would get better results if he was there on the ground speaking and meeting with fellow officers. Besides, they knew the area better than him and would cover more ground and suggest pathways and bridleways that maybe an out-of-town copper wouldn't know of.

Jess wanted to stay on the street in the open, the rain had stopped and it was dark but a mother's love is one of the most powerful forces in the world, nothing would stop her looking and if Toby was on foot, she would be too.

"Where are you going?" asked Jim.

"If Toby is coming from that way – she pointed towards the east – I'm going that way too, maybe we'll meet en route" Jess replied as she set off.

Celia looked at Brian and shrugged, "she makes a good point, Toby might be another day away but we can reduce that by setting off towards him".

"But what if he's behind us? What if he caught another bus and is already in Weston? We'll be walking away from him" Brian argued.

"He's walking" Jess said convinced.

"We thought that before, we were a day behind, how do we know we're not another day behind? He already knows he can travel by bus, if he's done it once, he can do it again." Brian walked towards Jess.

"So what do you suggest we do?"

Cath and Jim stood looking at Brian and Jess, they were ten yards apart and arguing in the street, it was clear that emotions were running high and, if not properly planned, it could spill over and stupid decisions could be made. As ever, the voice of removed reason, Celia piped up.

"Let's make a plan, if you go off that way, and you're welcome to, he's your son, you might end up lost and alone in the dark too. You don't have any supplies, those are dark roads, anything could happen. I don't think it will hurt to take ten minutes to come up with an idea."

Emma, was close by listening to the group, this was dangerous, so many people with conflicting, yet well intentioned, ideas. She began cursing Craig beneath her breath, they would listen to him. Somehow, he'd led this group here and they clearly trusted him, what would Craig do?

"Let me phone Craig, he may have heard something from the local police" she offered.

Jess looked at Emma and thought for a second, she was right, they were all right, she was being impulsive, but she wanted Toby back safe and sound.

"Ok, call him. We'll go from there." She said reluctantly.

Emma called Craig and hoped he had an idea.

A cackling magpie woke Toby from his sleep, the sun was threatening to come up but the day was cold and damp, he had slept like a log but now he felt chilled, hungry and very alone. He stumbled from the cart still in his sleeping bag and started to light a fire but everything was too damp and he could hardly feel his fingers so decided to not bother. He packed up his things as quickly as he could, relieved himself against the side of the billboard and started moving, soon his body warmed up and his feet received some warmth, he glugged at his water bottle and started unpeeling one of his bananas, he would eat the eggs when the sun came up and he found a warm spot to rest.

Craig had told the group to split up and walk the length of St. George, one group on one side of the road and the other group would tackle the other side. The local police had told him they would make some

phone calls to the farmers and businesses on the approaching roads and Craig got in touch with the bus company to see if any passengers met Toby's description. Jess wasn't happy with the decision but at least she was busy, busy kept her mind from wandering and coming up with bad possible outcomes for Toby's welfare.
The town was only a few miles long, after a few laps the group grew tired and, after Emma's advice, rested in their cars at the entrance. No sign of Toby.
A few hundred metres away, Toby was sat eating his boiled eggs, the sun was coming through the leaves of some trees and Toby was staring at his map at the upcoming town. St. George was bigger than anywhere he'd visited on this journey, was it too big, he wondered if he'd be seen by someone and his trip would be over. He'd spent two nights on the road and it would be so sad if it all ended here. Maybe there was another way. He looked at the map and suddenly a name caught his eye; Canada.
There was another Canada. To the south. He could bypass St. George and head towards a place called Lower Canada, if there was anywhere that could make him avoid his friends name it would be his dad's home. He made the decision in a few seconds; he was off to Canada.

"Ok, here's the plan, we head towards Bristol from here, I've heard nothing back from the bus companies, the police are still making enquiries to local businesses and homes along Toby's route but, the truth is, he's been out two nights now, that's too long, we need to find him now." Craig was blunt and his words surprised him, was he now thinking the worst and was worried for the boy? He had faith in the little chap but two days is a long time for someone to be out without food and water. The last thing he wanted was to find him injured or in a ditch by the side of the road having been hit by a vehicle.
"I said this last night!" Jess said.
"Last night it was dark, it would have made everything doubly hard to find him. I think he's camping at night and walking in the day, I

can't see how he's sticking to roads, someone would have seen him and reported it, so he must be on paths or fields, either way we wouldn't see him unless we were on the ground so I think we split into three teams. Jim and Cath go by car and patrol the road, stay in touch by phone. Jess, you go with Emma and I, we'll head out on foot now and hopefully meet him along the road or on one of the paths, Brian, you go with Celia and follow us out a minute or two behind, if we miss him the chances are you'll see him." Craig grabbed some things from his car and started getting ready.

Jess was chomping at the bit.

"We head as far as Redhill, that's about four miles, and then head back, if we meet Brian and Celia on our return journey, we'll think of taking some side roads."

Craig looked at the group, they were tired but ready.

"Let's go."

Toby had a newly-found motivation, his route had found him walking alongside a helicopter museum and the sunshine made his journey more fun than usual, he was getting used to the routine of walking, eating, walking, eating, walking, camping, sleeping and repeat. Along the way he would find things to eat to add to the meagre supplies he was able to get before he left, but a small boy needs small food, he was thankful that he didn't have to feed and water a horse on this journey. Of course, his trip would have been a fraction of the time and effort but finding food for one was easier than finding food for one and a horse.

Lower Canada was nothing like the Canada his dad told him about, he knew it wasn't going to be the same, the Canada he knew of was across the ocean and had bears, ice hockey and police officers in red coats and cowboy hats, this was a village not a vast expanse of land north of the USA. Once he was in, he was already leaving.

The next stop was the Weston Super Mare hospital, it was signposted and easy to reach, one long road (he even had time to nip into a shop and buy some bananas, peanuts and some bottles of water – he stayed close to a single woman in the shop to create the

illusion of them being related) and it brought him a feeling of pride when he kept seeing the name of his destination.
Soon this would be over, soon he would find his old foster family and he would ask them if he could stay with them for a while. It was a great plan; his mum would join them once Dean was out of the picture and they could stay there until she thought of their next step. Maybe they could move to Canada to live nearer his dad and Celia, she seemed nice, maybe his mum and her could be friends and they would make a new family in a new country. He'd miss Jim and Cath but they could visit. Nothing was impossible.

"I don't know how he's done it, but he's just not here" Craig said to the group.
They were in a layby at the side of the road a mile or two outside of St. George. Emma had had her phone glued to her ear all day in the hope that something would come up about his whereabouts, this was useless, they were searching a large area and it seemed no one had seen him. He'd disappeared.
"Didn't we take Toby here one summer?" Brian asked Jess.
"Hmm?" Jess answered.
Brian pointed to the billboard behind them, "the soft play place, it had those animals you could feed".
Jess looked up, "Yeah I think so."
Jim walked behind the billboard, it seemed as good a place as any to have a toilet break.
He came back around to the group, "come and look at this!" he shouted.
The group followed him to find someone had made a fire behind the board, there was an empty tin can on the floor next to some sticks.
"Toby" Jess and Brian said in unison.
"He's been here" Craig said amazed.
"Recently too, it's dry, if it was before yesterday wouldn't it be wet?" Emma asked.
Brian nodded, this was it, his son had made it all the way here. They'd only just missed him.

"But the map said he was going to St. George, why did we not see him? We've been up and down here all day." Cath started looking up and down the road in the hope that he was still nearby.

"Well let's think logically, - Emma grabbed the map – we're around here, so where would he have gone?"

The group looked at the map, no logical or sensible route jumped out, the only sensible route was the one through St. George, the direct route.

"He was worried about being seen" Jess announced.

"Yeah, perhaps he diverted another way" Brian added.

"But which way? – Craig asked looking closer at the map – did he go north or, oh hang on" Craig looked at Brian.

"You moved to Canada, right?" He asked.

"That's right – Brian replied – we live in Vancouver"

"He's gone south" Craig showed the map to Jess.

"Oh my god!" Jess said smiling.

"He's gone to Canada!" Emma laughed.

They gathered around and saw the name on the map.

Jess was already making her way to the cars, Toby was within grasp, she could feel it, she was shaking with excitement.

Chapter Seventeen – Supper on The Beach

The first thing to hit Toby was the smell. The coastline of England has a certain scent to it, a mixture of salt, sand and the smell of the ocean, eventually vinegar and cooking oil is added to the cocktail as a hundred restaurants cook up the fish and chips for the tourists. Toby made his way past a golf club and a row of three storey houses that stand facing the sea, he could hear seagulls and hear the noise of people visiting the seaside town. His legs were tired, luckily the cart was easier to pull along the flat seafront, he dodged people walking their dogs, skateboarders and elderly people driving mobility carts. If he has to make the return journey, he thought to himself, he'll use one of those, they go quite fast and it would be done in half the time. He would drag the cart behind like a trailer.

He could see people riding donkeys on the beach, someone was flying a huge kite, footballs being kicked, children using buckets and spades to build sandcastles, parents applying sun cream and laying out towels to sit on. There was no shortage of people enjoying the sunshine. What a place.

He reached the pier; it was so busy and he heard people tutting as they had to avoid him hitting them with the cart. Nearby was an old-style carousel, brightly painted carved wooden horses went around and around and up and down as old Victorian music played. If he could find a safe place to park his cart, he'd ride on it.

There were groups of people coming and going, some eating ice cream, some washing their sandy feet under a tap by public toilets, young children crying, seagulls swooped for rogue chips, there was a tiny train that went back and forth along the seafront and that smell of fried fish, all amazing things for a seven year old to experience. There were dogs everywhere, big dogs, small dogs, fluffy dogs with shiny collars, dogs in little pushchairs, dogs tied to those mobility carts trotting alongside their owners and there were groups of dogs. Toby saw a dog that looked like Lizzie, the police dog, it was sniffing the ground and moving towards him. Its owner was a tall man that looked a little like Craig from a distance, he was obscured by passers-by but it looked like him. Close behind was a man resembling his dad!

"Dad!" Toby shouted.

"Dad! Dad!" Toby started to walk, the cart dragging behind him. Suddenly his dad looked his way, "Toby!" he bellowed, he looked to a woman nearby and said something, Toby couldn't believe it, it was his mum. His mum was here with his dad, and there was Emma, and Jim and Cath! He could see another woman who he knew was Celia. Toby dropped the handle and broke into a run, his eyes watered as his small feet pounded the floor, any pain in his legs had gone as he saw his parents run too.

His mum was first there, she scooped him up and held him so close, she pulled him tighter and he could feel her tears in his hair.

"We're at the seaside!" Toby said.

Craig stood back and felt a little emotional at the scene, people had parted leaving an open space in the middle of the promenade.

"Well that was easy" Emma said to Craig.

"Yeah, it was wasn't it" Craig smiled.

Brian, Toby and Jess all hugged – even Harold was included after a few dogs sniffed in his direction as they passed. It's difficult to describe that feeling of being reunited with something that is simply a part of your being. You sense the piece is missing, everything seems wrong while its gone, but when it's returned, everything makes sense.

Near the carousel sits a group of girls, probably ten or eleven years old, still wearing their school uniforms. They meet most days after school and share some chips and chat about things. They grew curious when a little boy ran screaming across the seafront into the arms of, presumably, his parents. It was an odd show, there were lots of adults and this one child – and a dog. They discussed what they were watching, perhaps the little boy ran off and he's been found, maybe this is someone they haven't seen for a long time or maybe this was a group from the local 'funny farm' who had taken a shining to the young boy. Who knew? No one seemed to be in any danger and they all seemed happy enough with what was going on. But there was something about the boy.

One of the girls looked at the boy, did she know him? He looked familiar but she didn't know any boys like him. She watched him as he was held tightly and kissed, and she saw the stuffed toy that was tucked beneath his arm. She used to know a boy that had a yellow rabbit like that, she was the one who gave it to him, but that was years ago. This couldn't be the same little boy; her foster carers, the Franks, told her he went to live with a couple soon after he arrived leaving her and the other children to get on with things.

"You ok Millie?" one of her friends asked as she stood up to leave. She replied in a smoky voice "yes I'm fine, just daydreaming I guess". She stood too, she took one last look at the reunion on the seafront and pulled her blonde ringlets into a pony tail and tied it back with a hair band.

"Fancy going to the shops again, before they close?" Another friend asked.

Millie nodded and smiled, she'd seen some things in her life, this was just something else to add to the long list, "could do – she replied – it's a bit of a trek though isn't it?"

The other girls laughed and walked off in the direction of the shops, the drama was over, there were shiny things to look at.

Toby spent the remainder of the day by the sea, he slowly understood why everyone was there and he was pleased when he heard his dad had punched Dean, all in all it was a pretty good adventure, the man on the television would be impressed.

Printed in Poland
by Amazon Fulfillment
Poland Sp. z o.o., Wrocław